A SHADOW MELODY

BRIAN KAUFMAN

Black Rose Writing | Texas

ISBN: 978-1-68513-100-5 (Paperback); 978-1-68513-136-4 (Hardcover)
PUBLISHED BY BLACK ROSE WRITING
www.blackrosewriting.com

Printed in the United States of America
Suggested Retail Price (SRP) $20.95 (Paperback); $25.95 (Hardcover)

A Shadow Melody is printed in Bookman Old Style

*As a planet-friendly publisher, Black Rose Writing does its best to eliminate unnecessary waste to reduce paper usage and energy costs, while never compromising the reading experience. As a result, the final word count vs. page count may not meet common expectations.

To Elinor Kaufman, who knew something about unconditional love.

A SHADOW MELODY

"In the depths of horror and despair, one comes to a new steadiness. There is no farther to fall."
~Winston Graham in *Ross Poldark*

"Love is the magician that pulls man out of his own hat."
~Ben Hecht

CHAPTER ONE

A Curious Apparatus/ Shadows on a Wall

Ohio, 1899

His father held his cap, twisting it like a dishrag. Seven-year-old Harry stood behind, staring up at George Browning's head. Without the cap, the man's bald spot was visible, making him look older. He appeared shorter as well, as if his slumped shoulders were pulling him down. When the front door opened, George asked for Miss Nesbit in a voice with more squeak than certainty. Invited over the threshold, Harry and his father stepped inside.

The entrance was grand. To the left, a stairway crept up the wall like a curved serpent. Overhead, the morning sun shone through huge windows, glistening in the crystals of a chandelier. An older woman made her way toward them from the front hallway, which stretched into the dark like a coal tunnel. Her stiff, floor-length gown hid the motion of her feet, so that she seemed to glide rather than walk. She stopped and urged them forward with a twitch of her finger. Harry's father shoved him ahead. Veering right after just a few steps, the woman led them back into the light.

The morning room was a cheerful space with bright, striped wallpaper, a loveseat, a roll-top desk, and a number of ornate wooden chairs. Miss Nesbit went to the desk and began to speak without looking at Harry's father.

"I've inspected your work and found it acceptable, Mr. Browning. Will a cheque be satisfactory?"

"Yes, your ladyship."

She glanced back. "None of that. I've told you."

"Sorry, ma'am." He gave the wool cap another twist. "Did you happen to notice the woodpile when you inspected the garden?"

"No. Is there something wrong with the woodpile?"

"Not at all, leastwise not now," he said. "The stacks were in some disarray, and a bit . . ." Here, he paused, as if searching for the right word. "Slender. They were slender."

"Has my wood lost weight, then?"

Harry's father gave a nervous chuckle. "A good one. No, the wood is plump as a partridge. At least, it is now. I took the opportunity to finish the chopping work someone else left behind."

Miss Nesbit's face, long and severe, grew sterner still. "I did not contract you to chop wood."

"No, ma'am, you did not. Still, a job's not done till the work around it is done. That's what I always say. I only mention it in hopes that you noticed and that it pleased you."

"As I said, I didn't notice." She turned back to the draft on her table.

George cleared his throat. "I also had hopes that you'd have other work for me."

She finished writing, picked up the cheque and blew lightly on the wet ink. Satisfied with her efforts, she handed it over. As he reached out, she met his gaze. "Your work was good. Come back next month. If I have anything for you to do, you will be welcome to it."

To Harry's young eye, the room was cluttered. The chairs were curved, ribbed, and delicately upholstered, as if only women sat here. Surely, anyone as large as his uncle Frank would snap them to kindling in the act of sitting. Floral curtains with pleated valances blocked much of the sun—the light replaced by a trio of wall sconces. A score of framed photographs hung in clusters on three of the walls. The fourth wall featured a marble fireplace so clean that it might never have been used. Several small tables throughout the room were festooned with vases and decorative plates. Harry thought of one of his father's frequent sayings. When supper consisted of half a bowl of stew or soup from the kettle and Harry wished aloud for a second helping, his father would answer, "Sometimes, less is more." Looking around the room, Harry finally found agreement.

So busy was the room, with its lime-colored rug and table doilies, that he almost missed seeing the apparatus. A simple, varnished wooden box hung on the wall, chest-high to his father with a black, conical microphone extending six inches from the middle of the box. On the side, an earpiece and cord dangled from a hook-switch. Near the top, a bell device.

Miss Nesbit turned to regard Harry. "It's a telephone, young man."

"He knows what a telephone is, ma'am" Harry's father said, his voice one tone lower than it had been a moment before.

"May I try it?" Harry asked.

"My goodness!" Miss Nesbit softened her stern expression. "No. At any rate, it's out of order. I expect someone from the plant to look at it later today, or perhaps tomorrow. Until then, it's quite useless."

Harry moved quickly, sliding one of the dark, walnut chairs to the base of the phone.

"Heavens!" Miss Nesbit's hands fluttered like birds escaping from a cage.

Harry climbed on the chair's upholstery. Popping the side latch, he swung open the cover of the apparatus and stared inside.

The mistress of the house squawked at him while his father grabbed him roughly and lifted him from the chair as if grabbing up a sack of flour.

"Harry! What were you thinking?" His father's voice had dropped to a low growl.

"It's not broken," Harry said.

"What on earth?" Miss Nesbit asked.

"It's not broken," Harry repeated. "There's a wire loose."

George Browning set Harry on the floor and stooped in order to level his gaze. "Are you sure?"

Harry nodded.

"I'm sorry, ma'am," George said, standing up straight. "Dreadfully rude, it was. But Harry is usually right about such things. He has a knack."

Miss Nesbit glared at her chair, and then at Harry. "What wire, young man?"

"The talk battery is disconnected from the magneto."

Miss Nesbit recoiled as if she'd been slapped. She looked to his father, who shrugged and said, "He knows things," as if that explained everything.

"Are you saying that you fix this?" Miss Nesbit asked. "The man from the plant is supposed to be here later, so if you cannot, please say so."

"I can fix it."

"And you won't break it? Worse than it already is?"

Harry shook his head.

Miss Nesbit stepped back and held out an aged hand, gesturing to the chair. "Go ahead," she said. "You've already soiled the upholstery. I'll have to have it cleaned, of course."

Harry climbed up again and attached the conspicuously loose wire. He studied the inside of the telephone as if inspecting the rest of the parts, rather than memorizing—the latter being his true motivation.

"Is it fixed?" she asked.

Harry nodded. "Yes, ma'am." He reluctantly stepped down from the chair.

Moving the chair aside, Miss Nesbit picked up the speaker from its hook, activating the line. She stared through wide eyes at George. "Your son is clearly afternoonified!"

George Browning smiled. "I told you he was smart."

She shifted to the front of the apparatus and spoke tentatively into the microphone. "Can you hear me?" she asked.

George squeezed his son's shoulder.

"Well. Well! Please, will you say hello to someone for me?" Miss Nesbit listened for a moment and then nodded. Stepping back, she held out the speaker. "Come say hello," she told Harry, the hint of a smile on her face.

"I'll do this," George said, grabbing the boy under his arms and lifting him to the wall phone. Harry placed the speaker against his ear and spoke into the cone. "Hello?"

"Hello," came the answer. Someone miles away was talking to him through the wires! The sound was thin and distant, but he could make out the word without difficulty. A wonder. A miracle.

"Where are you?" Harry asked.

The woman at the other end of the line laughed. "Why, I'm here!" she said. "I'm right here."

•   •   •   •   •

Though his father had gone to the bank to cash Miss Nesbit's cheque, dinner was soup from the night before, made bountiful once again with added water. Harry thought, less is not *always* more, but kept the joke to himself. His father was in an angry mood, staring into his emptied bowl, brows furrowed and mouth turned down. At last, he said, "A new century begins next year. We need a fresh start. Perhaps we'll move east. Your uncle Frank can get me work in the mines."

Harry's heart dropped. He liked Ohio and did not want to move. Fall was coming, and he yearned for the cooler nights and the changing of the leaves. "You hate the mines."

"I do. I do hate the mines." George's shoulders drooped low. "Don't worry. They'll not make a breaker boy of you." The mines used young children to sort coal on conveyor belts. Harry's father wouldn't ask that of him. George looked up from his bowl. "I'm old for the mines, as well. They are a young man's game."

"You're not *old*." Harry knew better but would not yield the point. "Uncle Frank's friends were *old*."

"They were in their thirties. Too young to wrinkle and stoop. By now, they've probably all gotten the lung."

"Uncle Frank is alive," Harry argued.

"Uncle Frank has his wife's money to live on. You can't build a belly like that on a miner's wage. And since he hurt his back, he doesn't work at all."

"I wish you didn't have to work."

"If wishes were horses, then beggars would ride," George said. "As for me, I will spend my life on foot." He threw the piece of linen he used as a napkin on the table and stood up. "I need steady work, son. Piecemeal work means no meals for us. Piecemeal? No meal."

Harry's face brightened. His father was playing another word game. "Or meals in pieces. Pieces of meals."

"Meals in pieces . . ." George's voice trailed off. "No better than feces."

Harry howled with laughter. The very best jokes referenced farts or excrement. His father smiled and tousled Harry's hair. "I'm tired. I'm going to bed. I need to be out and about before dawn tomorrow. I heard the lumberyard needs some clean-up work. The same for you, son. Clean up around here in the morning."

"I'll clean up and clean down," Harry promised.

His father smiled, pausing at the bedroom door. "How did you know the parts of a telephone?" he asked.

"I think I saw a diagram once."

"You think?"

"I can remember the diagram. I can't remember where I saw it."

His father pursed his lips. "Well," he said at last, "you seem to remember the important parts."

•   •   •   •   •

Harry waited to join his father until the man was asleep, snoring. Harry was not tired and did not want to disturb his father's rest with questions, or his constant tossing and turning. Once asleep, George would not stir.

They had little money for candles, but the moon was bright, and Harry did not have to feel his way. He eased onto the lumpy mattress beneath the window and lay on his side, staring at the wall.

If he had to move east, to Pennsylvania, it would break his heart again. He was certain of it. His friends lived here.

His mother's sister, Aunt Evelyn, lived in town. Even the President, Benjamin Harrison, was born in Ohio. What did Pennsylvania have to offer but tunnels and shacks?

The bright moon cast shadows on the wall, so Harry busied himself by watching them. Dark shapes of black moved against a gray wall. Wind moaned through the cracks around the window, and shadows writhed in tandem with the sound.

His father had promised that Harry would not have to work in the mines. To spend the sunlight hours in the darkest tunnels, sopping wet, hunched over a conveyor belt for the sake of pennies? Worse, to watch the weight of the mines push his father down until his lungs were stoppered?

He tried to calm his thoughts. Wind and shadows were his only distraction.

One large shadow resolved itself into a shape more or less human, with long, dark tendrils dancing to one side, like a person with long hair whipping in the wind. The lines of the shadow became more defined. Her shape—for it was clearly a woman—was familiar to him. Her hair twisted and thrashed, but she stood still, fixed in place.

He stared, mesmerized by the motion of the shadow's hair.

Harry began to be afraid. This shadow was alive, and more, it was staring at him. *She* was staring at him. He dared not look away, lest she approach the bed and snatch him up. The wind moaned again, and the shadow appeared larger, as if it were closer.

Harry tried to close his eyes, but they would not close.

Now, the voice of the wind called to him, like the low moan of a wind instrument. A bass oboe, like the one traveling musicians played. The air danced with an electrical charge, as if hooked to a battery. A phone battery, of course. If the wall phone were here, he would call up the shadow and ask what she wanted.

But he already knew the answer. She wanted him.

His mother. The ghost of his mother.

"Is that you?" he asked. His voice was thin and distant. He could barely hear himself.

The shadow closed in like the mouth of a tunnel.

Harry screamed.

• • • • •

In the morning, George walked Harry to the yard outside the bedroom window. The sun had risen an hour earlier, but he'd stayed home, having abandoned the thought of finding work at the lumberyard in favor of a few hours of uninterrupted sleep.

His son had fared no better during the night. Perhaps the excitement of the telephone put him on edge. More likely, the news that they might soon have to move disturbed him. Winter loomed, and they had no money left. Opportunities for work would be less, not more, when the snow began to fall.

He stopped to point at the willow tree. "See?" he asked. "The moon hid directly behind this tree, casting shadows on the wall. Look at the branches. They are thin as whips. What you saw was the tree and branches tossed by the wind. Not a ghost."

Harry stared at the tree, and then turned to look at the bedroom window. The wall with the shadow was in perfect line with the window and the tree. The truth of his father's words seemed to hit home. "I was dreaming. Or half-asleep." Harry nodded to himself, apparently satisfied.

George smiled. The boy was smart. "You see, Harry, if you think about it, most everything in the world has an explanation. You must reason your way to that explanation."

Harry frowned.

"What are you thinking?"

"Was there a reason Mother died?" Harry asked. His face was blank, so it was impossible for George to guess his intent. Were Harry a decade older, he'd guess he was being tested or perhaps taunted. But the boy was only seven.

"Only God can answer that question," George said. "It's not for men to know."

There was a cause of death, of course. Cholera. Tens of thousands of people had died from the "blue dream" over the course of the previous decade. Mary Browning had been confined to bed and treated with spearmint and camphor, all to no avail. But reasons? There were no reasons. George draped an arm over Harry's shoulders. "You miss her, don't you?"

"Yes." Harry said, his voice tentative.

"What are you thinking now?"

"I am having trouble . . . remembering her face."

George sighed. "Harry. She died four years ago. You were *so* young. It's natural to forget." He turned the boy to face him. "That doesn't mean you don't love her."

"Yes, it does," Harry said. His expression had shifted suddenly, as if he were about to cry. "You said that I remember the important things. You said it last night. Her face is supposed to be important."

"Now, now," George said, searching for the right thing to say. When he found it, he smiled. "Her face is important, but not as important as her heart. And you remember her heart."

For the second time that morning, something George said hit home with his boy. "Yes," Harry agreed. "Yes, of course. You're right. I will never forget her heart." Tugging free, he ran off as if the troubles of the previous night had never happened. George watched for a while as Harry kicked leaves in the distance. Then, he gathered himself for a trip into town, hoping the foreman of the lumberyard would still speak with him.

CHAPTER TWO

A Job Well Done/The Library

Ohio, 1899

While his father looked for work in town, Harry cleaned house and prepared dinner. He picked a handful of tiny carrots and a single celery root from the garden at the side of the bungalow. He boiled the carrots while cleaning the celery root bulb—stripping off the rind and the tentacle-like roots. He sliced the remains and set them aside. When the carrots were limp, he pushed them through a strainer.

Butter was a luxury they could not afford. Instead, Harry took a dab of fat from the coffee can and put it in a skillet, adding a spoon of flour. Then he stirred in the carrot paste all at once, rather than adding it a bit at a time. Cooking the right way took too long. The day waited without patience for him.

The soup was lumpier than it should have been, but it would do. His father would not complain.

Harry moved the cast iron skillet to a cooler spot, topping the mess with slices of celery root before capping the pan. He left the slices to steep like tea, adding a hint of the missing butter flavor to the dish. Had he been able to bake bread with any consistency, he would have done so, but the wood oven was his enemy, wasting too much of the family's flour.

His father had not yet returned from town, which meant that he either found work, or stopped at the tavern.

Either way, the afternoon belonged to Harry. He resisted the urge to taste the tiny batch of soup. The cupboard held walnuts and a chunk of broxy—market meat rinsed in vinegar to ward off disease. He took some of each and raced outside.

The day was bright and crisp, with a hint of sour apple in the breeze. He ran to the crest of the hill and looked down into the village, which sprawled a half mile below. So many small houses, some within a hundred feet of each other! His father said there were too many—that Ohio was becoming like Philadelphia, where people lived on top of each other, stacked like boxes. Harry imagined being on the bottom of the stack, crushed flat, and laughed. His father liked to exaggerate. If true, Harry would simply shrug and roll away, letting them all tumble to the ground.

To the left of the village stood the church and the graveyard where his mother was buried. The sight made his heart stumble, and for a moment, he forgot not to cry. Then he remembered that he was already seven years old and wiped his cheeks. Mother had been gone for a long, long time. Years. Still, he wished he could see her again.

Then he thought of the willow tree and decided to think about something else entirely.

In the brush ahead, where his father would never look, Harry had hidden a homemade spear. He retrieved the spear—four feet of tree limb with a sharpened end—and set about hunting. He crouched as he moved along the hillcrest. The lower to the ground he was, the less likely he'd be seen.

Wouldn't it be a surprise if his father found a cutlet from a white-tailed deer next to his carrot soup? Harry hadn't seen a white-tail since the last of the forest had been cleared, nor did he know how to butcher a felled deer, but he could pretend. Hunting was fun. He'd never killed anything (secretly wondering if he even could) but creeping around with a spear was a fine way to spend the afternoon. He made sure to take notice of the sun. When it was time for supper, he'd heat the carrots and celery root, and wait for his father's return.

•   •   •   •   •

When George came home, Harry had restarted the wood stove and placed food on the table. His father was neither angry nor jovial, and he did not smell of spirits, so he'd clearly gone to work and not to the tavern. His father put a spoon to the carrots without comment, seeming to think through a question, as if furrowing one's eyebrows somehow focused one's mental prowess.

Harry furrowed his own brows until his father noticed.

"What are you thinking?"

"The soup. Is it good?"

"It's delicious," George said, chewing with sudden zest.

In truth, the soup was abominable—all lumps and paste. Harry was hungry—always hungry!—but he cleaned his bowl without wishing for seconds.

When his father finished eating, he cleared his throat and said, "I have some news. I have work tomorrow."

"At the lumberyard?"

"No, though the lumberyard has much to do with what might be a change in fortune. When I arrived, the work was half done, but the foreman was keen to finish the clean-up and put me on for a half day. While I was working, I noticed a gentleman watching us. The gentleman said something to the foreman and pointed at me."

"Was he a policeman?"

George snorted. "No. He was the owner of the lumberyard, and he liked my work. He asked if I cared to do some chores around his home, and of course, I said yes. Tomorrow, we go to New Concord. It's an hour on foot, so we'll have to be up early." He paused. "Or would you rather stay here?"

"I'm going,' Harry said.

•   •   •   •   •

The walk took nearly two hours, in part because Harry got tired. George stopped twice, letting Harry sit, once by the side of the road, and once on the banks of a small creek. By the time the sun came up, New Concord came in view, and Harry found his energy restored. The lumberyard's owner lived on the east side of town, closest to the road, so they arrived on time despite themselves.

George began by clearing leaves from gutters and checking the eaves for rain damage. Harry held the ladder, though had it slipped sideways, Harry would have been hard pressed to prevent a disaster. By noon, George had circumnavigated the house, and Mr. Brympton—the owner of the manor house and lumberyard—came to see what his new hired man had accomplished.

Brympton was a stocky but otherwise fit sort of man with a full beard, perhaps more closely trimmed than was the fashion, dressed in waistcoat, plain white shirt, and black trousers. He spoke with some friendliness to George, and by listening, Harry learned that Brympton taught languages at nearby Muskingum College, as well as tending his lumber business.

In mid-conversation, Brympton considered Harry, a puzzled look on his face. "Is this your son?"

"Yes. Harry, say hello to Mr. Brympton."

"Hello," Harry said.

"I'd have thought you'd be in school," Brympton said.

"Second term doesn't start until November," George explained.

Brympton nodded. "Well, a young man needs nourishment to keep an active mind." He turned toward the front entrance and pointed. "Go through the main hall to the back of the house. When you get to the kitchen, tell Cook that I sent you. Mrs. Beckwith makes cakes that will eventually be the death of me." He patted his stomach. "But you are a young man, and if you walked all the way here this morning, you have a fine constitution. You will likely survive her baking."

Harry stared without moving.

Brympton turned to George. "Is that all right with you, Mr. Browning?"

George nodded, licking his lips. Harry headed for the front door, resolving to bring something back for his father.

The front hall was dark—all polished wood and somber portraits. Mr. Brympton's ancestors—all of them looked like Brympton—as portrayed in oils, were a sturdy, serious lot. One man, thinner than the others, wore a clerical collar. His nose hooked like an eagle's beak. A woman dressed in white struck Harry as terribly plump, taking the full breadth of a loveseat. She carried the same subdued expression as the other portrait subjects, as if her girth had drained her mirth. "A dearth of mirth," Harry whispered, grinning. He would have to tell that one to his father.

That was when he passed the open door of the library. The room, larger than Harry's home, held shelves and shelves of books, from floor to ceiling. Bookcases ringed the perimeter, interrupted only by the occasional painting or framed map. There were hundreds—maybe millions!— of books. Harry stepped inside. The room was hushed as a chapel. Harry could smell dust and a hint of mold, but also, sawdust and vanilla. A single chair, thick-legged and sturdy, sat next to a small, round wooden table. Both pieces were polished, but otherwise unadorned. Harry crossed the room and sat down on the chair without so much as a squeak. Solid. Not fancy, like Miss Nesbit's furniture, but trustworthy.

Jumping up again, he crossed over to the nearest bookshelf. He reached out to take down a volume, but his hand hung in the air. Which book? he thought, as if he'd gone to a harvest feast, hungry, and found dozens of dishes perfectly prepared. How could he choose? He closed his eyes and extended his hand.

Backing away, the book clasped to his chest, he returned to the chair and began to read.

·　　·　　·　　·　　·

Brympton stopped in the open door of his treasured library—his sanctuary—staring at the boy in his chair. Impertinent young man! He'd sent him to the kitchen without an escort, and he'd apparently made the most of the accommodation! He started to speak but stopped himself when he noticed that the boy had not looked up. Brympton leaned against the doorframe and watched as Harry flipped pages. Surely, the boy was looking for pictures. No little boy could read so fast. His father was clever enough—he'd revealed that much in conversation. But the boy? What was he up to?

Brympton cleared his throat.

No response.

Brympton asked, "What have you got there?"

Young Harry looked up, startled. His stricken expression amused Brympton, though he did not allow himself to show as much. "You've helped yourself to my books, I see."

"I'm sorry, sir." Harry closed the book—gently—and set it on the table. "I've never seen . . . *so many books*." He finished in a rush, his voice filled with awe.

Brympton tried very hard not to smile. "What were you reading?" he asked.

Harry glanced at the book's spine. "*Apology of Socrates*," he said.

"And what do you make of it?"

Harry bit his lower lip, and then said, "Socrates thinks that wisdom lies in knowing that you don't really know much at all."

Brympton started. "Well! That is as concise a précis as I've heard."

"What is a précis?" Harry asked.

"A summary. Do you know what that is?"

"Yes," Harry said, as if everyone in Ohio knew as much.

"Have you encountered this book before?"

"No. But it seems like a very good book."

Brympton was tempted to laugh, so he turned his head. When he had control of his face again, he turned back. "How old are you, Harry?"

"Seven," Harry said proudly. "I'll be eight soon."

How on earth did a seven-year-old develop that kind of understanding. "Did you ever reach the kitchen?"

Harry blushed. "No, sir."

Brympton nodded in sympathy. "Though you would not necessarily know it from looking at me, I have always preferred books to food. Tell me, from the perspective of a young man of your advanced age, do you agree with Socrates or disagree with him?"

Harry considered the question. "Neither agree nor disagree, sir."

Brympton smiled. "No opinion, then?"

Harry put a hand to his mouth as if to stifle a smile. "There are so many books here. I am reminded how little I know. I guess that makes me very wise."

Brympton guffawed despite himself. He pulled a handkerchief from his waistcoat and dabbed at his eyes. "Perhaps so, perhaps so," he said. He liked this boy. He seemed much the same as the father—kind and clever. But the boy was unusually bright. He wished that his students at the college were as sharp and engaged. He had already decided to add the elder Browning to the estate staff. He would insist that the father relocate so that the journey back and forth did not weigh against such a position. And he would make sure that, when not in school, the younger Browning would have access to the library. He'd seen the care with which the boy handled his books. He would need no great amount of direction. *Return the book to the spot from which you took it. Turn the pages carefully.* The boy would do as he was told.

Later, as George Browning made ready for the long walk home, Brympton took him aside and made him an offer. Browning pretended to consider, and then accepted graciously. "You will move here, to the estate," Brympton said.

"Oh! Really? Well, that's wonderful."

Had the man thought he'd have to walk back and forth? Perhaps he was just flustered. "I can send a wagon for your things," he offered. "Will Saturday be satisfactory?"

"Yes, yes," George said. "And my boy comes with me?"

"Of course," Brympton said. Browning was stumbling over his words—clearly nervous. "I assure you—we'll make young Harry quite at home. And," Brympton added, "he will be welcome to visit my library as often as he likes. He is quite the reader."

George pursed his lips as if to wonder what Harry had gotten into.

Meanwhile, Brympton took a deep breath, glanced at the darkening sky, and realizing that he'd tired of the conversation, waved the elder Browning away. "I will see you in a day or two, then."

·   ·   ·   ·   ·

"A million books," Harry said. "Or a billion."

"A trillion?" George asked.

"A quadrillion," Harry finished.

Stars filled the cold night sky. The moon lit their way. There would be no dinner when they reached home, but morning would be filled with excitement as they gathered their things and made ready for the move to New Concord. Pots and pans, clothing, a box of books, including Harry's favorites—Poe and Dickens. A few tools, and George's knife. If the one-eyed cat that sometimes came around for scraps was present when it was time to travel, Harry would try to coax him into the wagon.

"How did you find Mr. Brympton? Did you like him?" George asked.

"He's a very nice man," Harry said. "I think he's less sour than the rest of his family."

George looked down at his son as they walked. "Why would you think that?"

"The hallway leading to the library is full of paintings. Old people in fine clothing, all looking as if they'd chewed lemon rinds."

George laughed in the dark. "I hope you didn't say that to him."

20

"Of course not," Harry said. "It might make him feel bad."

"I pray this new position works out, Harry. If it does, we'll be able to stay here in Ohio. Not so far away from your mother, is it?"

"It's far. But not too far," Harry said.

Arriving at their bungalow, drained and happy, Harry crossed the yard, making a wide berth around the willow tree and heading inside for a well-deserved rest. George rustled through the cupboard and brought back a half-handful of nuts for each of them, along with a tall glass of water. Then, exhausted, they fell into bed.

Harry felt certain that he would soon be asleep. He would miss his home and his friends in the village. He would miss attending his mother's grave—though he could and would visit often.

He would not, however, miss the willow. He closed his eyes, resolute in his decision not to look at the evening's shadows.

CHAPTER THREE

A Tragedy/ Mr. Brympton's Proposal

Ohio, 1899-1903

Looking back, Harry would think of the following years as the happiest of his life. His father, no longer scrambling for employment, applied his diligent nature to the tasks of both gardener and groom. As such, he communicated directly with Mr. Brympton, though in theory, he took direction from both the head groomsman and the master gardener. The groomsman had begun his career as a postilion—guiding the lead-left horse for Brympton's carriage. Because of his experience (and his ambition), the groomsman was certain that the success of the manor rested squarely on his shoulders. Worse, he viewed George Browning as a threat to his ascendency. For those reasons, he was able to find fault with what was otherwise faultless work. By contrast, the gardener was an older man with a pleasant disposition who appreciated the expertise George brought to bear.

For Harry's part, the threat of moving east to the much-dreaded Pennsylvania had been removed. His father seemed happy, and they had plenty of food on the table. Mr. Brympton was a generous employer.

Foremost in Harry's heart, however, was the time he spent in Brympton's library. He attended both yearly sessions at the nearby school, and when he turned ten years of age, he began employment at the house as a hall boy under the supervision of the porter. In addition to the duties of an aspiring footman, he performed certain minor repairs, having proven himself to be adept in matters of gadgetry. When the carpenter's electric drill stopped working, Harry rewired it. When Brympton brought home a new invention—the electric vacuum cleaner—Harry kept the motor running. The remaining hours of his day were spent reading Mr. Brympton's books.

•　　　•　　　•　　　•　　　•

Brympton's library held an astonishing collection covering all disciplines. Though Mr. Brympton was a devout Presbyterian, in keeping with founders of Muskingum College, his library had a pronounced secular determination. One night, as Brympton ushered Harry from the house, the older man pointed at the moon and said, "You can only see one side, you know. The same side faces us at all times because the earth's rotation and the moon's orbit are synchronous. Do you ever wonder at what's on the other side?"

Harry nodded with enthusiasm.

"Luckily, matters of significance here on earth don't face the same restrictions. You can find out both sides of a matter if you wish to. If not, because you are lazy or predetermined toward one view, then half of the truth will always remain a mystery to you. Like the moon."

Brympton often stopped by the library to ask what Harry was reading. Upon discovering the subject of the day, he would tug thoughtfully at his immaculate beard or pat his belly—or both—and launch into a brief dissertation. On the topic of the sciences, he reminded Harry that an investigation into the nature of the universe was not always appreciated. "Women who experimented with herbal remedies were called witches and burned at the stake. Men who thought the earth revolved around the sun, rather than the other way around, were tried for heresy and forced to recant."

"Galileo Galilei," Harry said, nodding at the book in his lap.

"Yes, of course."

"We are more enlightened."

Mr. Brympton frowned. The boy in the chair spoke of enlightenment as if he were an adult. "Don't be so sure," Brympton warned. "Some speak of science as if it were a new and better religion, when it is nothing of the sort. It is a method. An inquiry." He tapped his chest. "I am a Presbyterian. Do you know what that means?"

"My father says it means that you're stubborn."

Brympton snorted and harrumphed. "Well, perhaps that's so." The boy was not smiling, but something in his attentive gaze made Brympton wonder if Harry was having a go at him. One could never tell with Harry. "Being a Presbyterian also means a belief in certain truths. The sovereignty of God. The virgin birth. The resurrection. Worldly knowledge is secondary."

"And yet, you have all of these books," Harry said.

Brympton grinned. "Yes, I do. Our maker fashioned me such that I have an inquiring mind. But that's neither strange nor uncommon. Think of it this way, Harry. God created the heavens and earth, and science studies the structure of that creation. Theologians and scientists have much in common."

Harry chewed at his lip for a moment. "But you said worldly knowledge was secondary."

"Yes. That's because I believe scripture contains the answer to every question of import."

"Then why did my mother die?" The question was delivered in a matter-of-fact sort of way, as if Harry had asked why gravity snatched apples from tree limbs.

There was no reason not to answer the question. "First Corinthians, chapter fifteen, verse fifty-six. *The sting producing death is sin.*"

"Are you saying my mother was bad?" Harry's gaze had narrowed, and an uncustomary hardness pursed his lips.

Brympton paused to consider. He was no stranger to a question like Harry's. Such questions were part and parcel of his vocation. But Harry was a boy. A boy he had come to deeply care for. When he spoke again, his voice was gentle. "Harry. Do you trust me?"

Harry blinked.

"Do you trust me?"

Harry nodded.

"Just as there are some matters into which science ought not delve, there are theological discussions that go beyond the scope of a young man's understanding—even one so brilliant as yourself. This is one of those discussions. I ask you to trust me in this matter. If you can do that, it will put your mind at rest. That is the singular blessing of faith."

Harry nodded.

Having extricated himself gracefully—at least, he hoped he had—Brympton bid Harry continue with his reading. Cook had been baking sweetbreads earlier, and Brympton was famished.

•　　　•　　　•　　　•　　　•

Shortly after his eleventh birthday, Harry was awakened by a knock at the door. He was surprised to discover he was alone, in the dark, slumped in his father's chair.

George had gone to the local tavern at sunset, planning to celebrate the end of another workday. He'd promised to return early. Harry stumbled across the room to answer the knock. Mr. Brympton filled the doorway, a lantern in his hand. The black night gave no other hint to the world outside, as if the earth itself had plunged into a mine shaft.

Harry began to shiver. Though the overcast night carried a touch of frost, Brympton's sorrowful expression was the cause of his chills. Without a word passing between them, Harry understood that his world had changed.

"I have bad news."

"Is he dead?" Harry asked. His voice was thin and dry as paper. "Is my father dead?"

Brympton nodded. "You will be strong, now." Harry swayed a bit, so Brympton put a hand on his shoulder. Harry steadied himself. "Good boy," Brympton said.

Turning, he motioned a scullery maid forward. The young girl, hidden from view behind the big man, stepped into Harry's quarters, bleary-eyed. "Annie will stay with you tonight. I am going to attend to some details that cannot wait." He reached out and patted Harry's shoulder again. "I'm sorry, Harry. You have been dealt a sorry hand. Annie will keep you company if you can't sleep, but I want you to try. Tomorrow will be soon enough to take stock of your situation."

Harry stared up at Brympton. "How did he die?"

Brympton turned to go.

"How did he die?" Harry repeated.

"He was killed," Brympton said. "Someone killed him."

"Then they have killed me, too," Harry whispered.

"Harry?" Brympton frowned.

Harry shook himself. "I am fine, sir."

Brympton stepped closer. "No, you are not, and you're not expected to be." He took a ragged breath. "I'll speak to you in the morning, Harry." He looked over to Anne, who stood slumped against the wall. "Take care of him," he ordered.

The girl gave a sleepy nod.

•   •   •   •   •

From the Brownings' quarters, Brympton traveled to New Concord's tiny police department, where the suspect in George Browning's murder had been jailed. George Browning had visited a local tavern, drinking and gambling over a game of skittles. Having won his match, he pocketed his tiny winnings and headed home, rather than giving his opponent a chance to regain his stake. This bad form was rewarded with a blow to the back of the head. George dropped facedown into the road—his skull broken. George's assailant, overcome with sudden remorse, went for help, but to no avail. Now, the man sat weeping in his cell, repeating George's name. They had been friends.

Brympton peered through the bars from the free side of the cell. "You've orphaned a child," he said.

"I know! I know! God help me!" Sanders—the man apparently had no first name—sat on the shelf that served as a cot, weeping.

Brympton pulled a handkerchief from his pocket and stuck it through the bars. "Good God, man! Wipe the snot from your face. You are a shambling mess."

Sanders took the linen and wiped his face. "What will I do?"

"Prepare yourself," Brympton said. "You will be tried, and then you'll be taken to the Ohio Penitentiary. There, you will be electrocuted."

The man flinched. "I'd rather be hung."

"Sinful men don't get to choose," Brympton said.

Sanders looked up. "Electrocuted, then. Does it hurt? Do you know?"

"Not for long," Brympton said. This was a lie. He'd heard tales of botched executions, complete with burning hair and exploding eye sockets. But there was nothing to be gained by frightening this pitiful man. "You have no children of your own?"

"No," Sanders said. "My seed dies with me."

"A wife?"

"She left me two years ago."

"You might still do some good in the world," Brympton said. "I know a fatherless boy who will need resources. What assets have you?"

"None," Sanders sobbed. "I own a watch, but it don't keep proper time. The boy is welcome to it. He can have my clothes as well."

Brympton shook his head and turned to go.

"Are you leaving?" The man's voice was shrill.

"I am," Brympton said.

•　　•　　•

The burial took place in the old churchyard, near where Harry's mother had been laid to rest. Brympton had asked for Harry's preference, and though at first, the boy seemed to have no preference for anything at all, he eventually asked that his father should be buried near his mother, rather than miles away in the New Concord cemetery. George Browning had never remarried, nor had he shown any interest in the widows or single women who might gladly have taken on the burden of a young son in exchange for a roof. As far as Brympton could determine, George Browning had missed his wife, so it was fitting that he be buried as close to her as possible.

Brympton paid for a plain, six-sided coffin rather than let George Browning be buried in a shroud. There had been a brief visitation the night before, so the staff could say their goodbyes. Because Browning's head had suffered considerable damage at the hands of his murderer, the coffin was nailed shut in advance. Those paying their respects filed into the front room of the manor, where candles lit the way. This, too, was unusual, for Browning was not a member of the family.

Brympton had insisted.

The morning of the interment, Brympton's carriage delivered them to the grave site. Arrangements had been made in advance. Though the spaces adjacent to the grave of Harry's mother were taken, Brympton secured a spot fifteen yards to the north, near a young oak tree. The weather was cheerful and crisp, in contrast to the somber mood of the party. Two men from town, one George's old drinking partner and the other a caretaker at the church, worked the coffin into the hole while Harry and Brympton waited. The local clergyman said words, none of which seemed to register with the boy. Then, Harry tossed a clod of dirt into the grave. As he waited, the caretaker began shoveling, and soon, the black earth had swallowed the coffin whole.

"We should talk about your future," Brympton said on the carriage ride back to New Concord.

"Will I be sent away?" Harry asked. He sat with his hands in his lap, swaying with the carriage as it moved along the dirt road.

"No, of course not," Brympton said. "But we do have some decisions to make, you and I." He sighed. Though he'd spent many hours talking to Harry about a wide range of topics, the discussions were always theoretical. Intellectual. This was different, and Harry's usual intensity seemed drained, like a dry cell battery gone dead. "You want to stay on, don't you?"

"Yes," Harry said. "If I leave, I won't be able to visit my family."

"I would hope that you could eventually think of . . ." Brympton's voice trailed off, and he winced. "I mean to say that I want you to consider the manor your home."

Harry started to speak but stopped short. They rode on in an uncomfortable silence for a while—Brympton turned to gaze out the window and Harry staring at his lap. Finally, Harry asked, "Will I be allowed to continue working?"

"Of course," Brympton said. "There's nothing wrong with learning to work. There's honor in it." He cleared his throat. "But I don't believe you were meant for service." Harry remained silent, so he continued. "You have a fine mind, Harry. As fine a mind as I've ever encountered." No response, but then, he'd asked no questions. "How do you imagine your future, Harry?"

"I don't know," the boy said with a voice so melancholy that Brympton nearly reached out to touch his shoulder.

"Here is a possibility," Brympton said. "Keep working at the manor, as before. Earn your keep, so to speak. Complete your studies at the school. You shall continue to visit my library, as well. When you are of proper age, we shall enroll you in the college where I teach. Muskingum College is an excellent institution. By then, you will have focused your attentions on one path or another. You will work hard, and you'll succeed. When you graduate, I will send you on your way, perhaps with a stipend to give you a proper beginning." He paused. "How does that sound to you?" This last, he delivered with a cheery turn of voice that fell flat as a flounder.

Harry tilted his head to regard Brympton, and then returned his attention to his lap. "Why would you?" he asked.

The question startled Brympton. He had expected almost anything else. He sat back in his seat, flummoxed. "I believe," he said, "that we are put on this earth for a purpose. I found my calling as a teacher. And you will be my finest student. God has given us both a great gift, Harry. It would be a sin to waste it."

More silence.

A sudden, gnawing certainty struck Brympton. The boy wanted something more from him. He closed his eyes for a moment and took a deep breath. "Besides, Harry, I quite enjoy our friendship. It would grieve me terribly to see it end."

The late afternoon sun cast the road in shadows. Brympton glanced at the boy and saw tears streaming down his face. Harry would not meet his gaze, but he leaned to his left, closer to Brympton, and when the carriage hit a rut, he slumped over against the large man's shoulder. There he stayed for the remainder of the journey home.

CHAPTER FOUR

A Curious Prank/High Expectations

Ohio, 1909

The bad news ran through the college like fire through a woodpile. John Knox Montgomery, the much beloved president of Muskingum College, had mangled his right hand cranking up his Hudson Model 20. The car's engine kicked back, and the crank handle cracked the man's hand. Depending on the student telling the story, Montgomery either lost four fingers, was crippled for life, or both.

In truth, he suffered several broken bones on the back of his right hand. In a cast and unable to muster the necessary strength with his left hand, he would be unable to crank start his roadster. It sat near the college, on display at the side of the road in front of Paul Hall. As each day of class ended, Montgomery passed the car, stopping to pat the bumper or check the tires before making his way home on foot.

This circumstance gave Harry an unexpected chance to shine. Among the students, much consideration had been given to various schemes and pranks involving the Hudson. One young man proposed painting the maroon car green, but since the president was almost universally admired, the idea was dismissed out of hand.

Harry had a different idea entirely, and his best friend Drew gladly followed any directions Harry gave him.

Andrew "Drew" Peterson, the Muskingum "Muskies" quarterback and captain of the football team, was a blond giant, standing a full two inches beyond six feet. Good-looking and naturally popular, he was nonetheless regarded as a humble, affable sort. His humility was well-earned—Coach Jones's team had lost four out of five games that fall.

An otherwise excellent student, Drew struggled with math—a subject in which Harry excelled. Tutoring sessions blossomed into a heartfelt friendship. Whereas some students shied away from Harry because of his intellect or his association with Mr. Brympton, Drew was fascinated by Harry. Both boys worked during the summer months, but spent quiet evenings fishing and talking, or hiking and talking. When Drew began dating Margaret, he insisted that Margaret's roommate Ruth go out with Harry.

The foursome became known in town as "the youngsters from the college up the hill." Saturdays consisted of dinner at the diner or a picnic at the gazebo in the square. New Concord boasted a motion picture house, and the quartet saw every new release.

Ruth was an attractive girl in a mousey sort of way, but Harry secretly adored Margaret. Bright and sassy, she possessed a beautiful singing voice and played the piano like a virtuoso. Harry's love of music found a focus in his best friend's girlfriend. However, his commitment to his studies and his friend Drew meant that his love for both music and the musician would go unrequited.

When Harry conceived of his plan for the Hudson, he did not inform the girls and swore Drew to secrecy. The idea was bold, though not without some attending danger.

Whether to bring the plan to fruition in the day or at night was a question of importance. President Montgomery's office was in the building attached to the rear of Paul Hall, with no view of the car. However, students would spot the boys in action, and perhaps report them. Working at night would be difficult. Lanterns would call attention to them just as surely as sunlight.

In the end, they decided to skip Sunday services and work through the morning. John Knox Montgomery was a dedicated Presbyterian, and the church was located on the far side of town. Students would be in church, so less likely to intervene.

No night lanterns meant no suspicious police.

Harry assembled the necessary parts over the course of a month. By the time he had everything he needed, the colors of autumn had given way to gray skies and cold winds. On the Saturday before putting their plan in action, the first snow of the season left four inches over New Concord. "It's going to be cold," Drew said.

"Fewer nosy people."

"I play football in this weather, but you're as thin as a soda straw."

"Don't worry," Harry assured him. "I'll be fine."

He wasn't, of course. He could not work the wires with mittens on, and his hands turned white as new snow within the first half hour. He'd come prepared—hot potatoes in both jacket pockets served as hand warmers— but a chill wind sucked the heat out of them in short order. Drew brought a ceramic hand warmer, but it cooled as well.

Having placed tools and parts on a blanket, Harry set about working. Like an assisting surgeon, Drew handed him what was needed. To keep his mind off his trembling hands, Harry explained each step. "Ford used a b-b-battery for his Model T," Harry said, his cold lips sputtering like an engine that would not turn over. "When the juice is gone, the batteries must be replaced. Like a f-f-flashlight. In theory, the crankcase of a running car should recharge the cells with enough spare power to run an electric lamp."

Drew cleared snow from the grass with his mittens and dumped the parts into a pile.

"What are you doing?" Harry asked.

"Shut up," Drew answered, smiling. He draped the blanket around Harry's shoulders. "How long will this take?"

"I could cut the time in half if my icicle fingers would cooperate." He pointed. "This here is a Bosch magneto. Best in the business. But the system is still dangerous."

"I heard the crank took President Montgomery's hand off."

"It was his arm," Harry said. "His entire arm. The overrun mechanism failed, and the crank spun around and around with Montgomery's arm attached to it. Students passing by thought the car was waving at them."

Drew burst out laughing. "You are a dilly. But I heard the engine backfired."

"Then our esteemed president was nearly killed by a car fart," Harry said. "Perhaps someone put fruit and cheese in the gas tank."

Drew covered his eyes, shaking his head. "A fart joke? A new low, Browning."

"Nonsense," Harry said, "Fart jokes are a time-honored tradition, dating back to the Sumerians."

"Bull."

"No, it's quite true," Harry said, tying off another wire. "The first fart joke was recorded somewhere around 1900 B.C." His blanket slipped to the ground. Drew bent down, retrieved the blanket, and returned it to his friend's shoulders. "I'm nearly done," Harry promised.

A voice startled them. 'And what are you gentlemen doing? Drew?"

Harry turned to find Margaret Harper looking smart in a fur hat and muffler.

"Harry Browning, what have you gotten my boyfriend into?" She had her lips pursed just so.

"I'm introducing him to a life of crime," Harry said.

"I don't doubt you for a moment," Margaret said. "But I should warn you both that Mr. Montgomery, LL.D. is walking this way to check on his car. Will the roadster still run now that you've had your way with it?"

"I'm not done with the lamp," Harry growled. He bent to the task, muttering and shivering while Drew whispered an explanation to Margaret. "Really?" she said, loud enough for Harry to hear. "If the Hudson company couldn't do that, why would you think Harry could?"

"Because he's Harry." Drew glanced up the road. In the distance, he saw a figure trudging through the snow. "The president's coming, Harry."

"I'm almost done," Harry said. He'd have already finished if his hands weren't turning blue. He rubbed them together for a moment, then bent to his task again. Behind him, he heard the president's shoes crunching in the snow.

"Gentlemen," President Montgomery said, his cast hand dangling at his side—fingers evident, despite the rumors. "Miss Harper? What brings you out in this frigid weather?" His voice had the sonorous quality of a minister, mixed with a hint of foreboding, as if he were about to launch into a sermon regarding the Day of Judgement.

"Done," Harry said, standing. He'd been squatting for so long that he was unsteady on his feet for a moment, and he leaned on the Hudson's bumper for support.

President Montgomery turned his stone gaze to Harry's hand, and Harry removed it at once.

"I assume an explanation is forthcoming," the president said.

"A demonstration should suffice," Harry said, though if he'd miscalculated, an explanation would surely follow. He cleared his throat and pointed at the president's cast. "An unfortunate accident," he said. "With your right hand compromised, starting your Hudson is *problematique*." He turned to Drew, as if to explain. "From the Greek, *problēmatikos*."

"I'm charmed and amazed," Montgomery said. "I'm also cold. If you have something to demonstrate, please proceed."

Harry nodded. "Step this way," he said, pointing to a button. "Push this," he said.

"You've drilled into my car?"

"You will thank me," Harry said. "Push the button."

President Montgomery reached across with his left hand and pushed the button. The engine coughed and then fired.

"Now, the button below it."

The president leaned in, squinting in the late afternoon gloom. He reached out and pushed the second switch. Harry had replaced one of the automobile's gas lamps with an electric one. The beam lit the road, glistening in the snow.

President Montgomery stood silent.

"The battery will eventually need to be replaced, but for now, it is recharging, with enough extra power to run the lamp. I connected a low-tension winding to the battery voltage—"

"You did this for me," President Montgomery said. It was a statement, not a question.

"Yes," Drew said.

"We thought you could use a hand," Harry added, "the one being damaged, and all."

Margaret gasped. A small twitch tugged at the corners of the president's mouth. "And how do I replicate this miracle of yours?" he asked.

"These are push button light switches, adapted for this use. The top one fires the engine, and the bottom turns on the lamp once the engine is running."

President Montgomery shivered. "As I said, I'm cold, gentlemen. I believe I will drive my Hudson home." He turned to Margaret. "Miss Harper, would you and your friends like a ride?"

"I have tools to take care of," Harry said. He took the blanket from his shoulders, spread it out on the bare spot in the snow, and began piling tools and leftover parts in the center.

The president of the college eased himself into the Hudson, careful not to strike his cast. Drew helped Margaret into the back seat and then slid beside her. Harry climbed in front, his pile of tools in his lap. Snow had begun to fall again, and the flakes shone in the headlamp. "Look how beautiful," Margaret said.

President Montgomery nodded in agreement. He put the car in gear with some difficulty, and then eased forward. He smiled. "It gets dark very quickly here in the north," he said. "This lamp is quite powerful." He sighed.

Drew leaned closer and said, "Your Hudson rides smooth."

"Thirty-two-inch wheels," Montgomery said. "Springs at both ends. The wheel spokes are second-growth hickory. Hard as iron."

"Spoken like a salesman," Harry said. "Sir."

President Montgomery frowned. He turned right at the bottom of the hill. "Miss Harper, I believe you live just a block or two from here."

"Yes, sir."

"Well, I'll drop you off first. That way, I can have a word with the boys."

After Margaret had been delivered safely to her doorstep, Montgomery drove one more block and then stopped. Turning back, he said, "I wonder if you boys understand that you do not drill into another man's property without his permission."

Neither Harry nor Drew answered.

"Your intent aside, there are principles involved. I would have thought that any Muskingum boy would understand that." Despite the approaching season, the president was clean-shaven. He scratched his bare, wrinkled chin and said, "There will be no consequences, gentlemen. Nor will there be a repeat performance. Am I understood?"

Both boys agreed.

Dropping Drew at his home, he added, "Will you be playing quarterback next year, Mr. Peterson?"

"Not if we go one-and-four again," Drew answered.

"Well, I'm sure you'll do better with another season under your belt. You're a fine lad. Go on, now." Drew bowed gallantly and strode to his porch.

Harry and the college president drove on in silence. The roadster had an open-air carriage—the Hudson Model 20 was a summer touring car. Cold wind laced with ice blew straight into their faces. Harry hunched his shoulders and prayed for the end of the ride.

Harry did not have to provide directions to the manor. Brympton had hosted faculty get-togethers in the past, and Montgomery always attended. He stopped at the entrance to the driveway without entering the grounds. Harry gathered his bundle and stepped from the car.

"Mr. Browning?"

Harry stopped.

Montgomery pointed at the starter button. "Is this a system of your own design?"

"Yes, sir."

"You have a remarkable mind, Mr. Browning. I will be surprised—indeed, disappointed—if you do not join ranks with the likes of Misters Edison and Tesla." He smiled, adding "Thank you for my electric starter."

CHAPTER FIVE

The Garden/ Abyssus Abyssum Invocat/ A Letter

Ohio, 1918

The April morning air was cold enough to turn Harry's breath to vapor, but Mr. Brympton insisted on sitting in the garden. He was still Brympton—stubborn and stoic—and the garden was his choice, even with snow covering the ground. Swallowed in blankets, the old man looked frail. The garden was still. Cold air dampened the songs of the robins and killdeers. In the distance, New Concord lay silent.

"I'm glad that your friend is going with you," Brympton said. Drew Peterson had enlisted with Harry. "You can look after each other."

"I believe they'll send us overseas together. Neighbors fight well alongside neighbors."

Brympton snorted. Harry knew the sound and cherished it, even though it usually signified disagreement. "Are you cold?"

"No, no. Springtime is coming. I can smell it."

"Actinomycetes," Harry said, grinning.

Brympton smiled at the mention of soil bacteria, but the smile did not last. He sank down into his blankets. When he spoke again, his voice was huskier than before. "I wanted to say a great deal before you left, but the words seem to have left me."

Harry shook his head. "We don't need to speak. We can just sit here."

Brympton nodded.

The sky was gunmetal gray—heavy and dank. Easier to believe that snow would fall than to expect the crocus and snapdragons to blossom.

"There is something I do need to tell you," Harry said. "You can just listen."

"Nothing ruinous, I suppose," Brympton said. "We've always been candid with each other."

"Yes. But there is one thing left to say." Harry took a deep breath. "I can never repay you—"

Brympton cut him off with a wave. His hand hung in the cold air for a moment, fingers curling, then brushed a single tear from his cheek before ducking back under the blanket.

After a while, Harry continued. "I've led a blessed life. I can't thank my mother or father for their love. They're gone. I can thank you, and do so with all of my heart, but I can't repay what you've done for me." He looked away. If he met Brympton's gaze, he would not be able to continue. "You asked me not to volunteer. I want to explain why I did so, despite your disapproval. My luck, my blessings, include the country where I was born. Enough commerce exists here to build a simple life with a family of one's own, as my father did. If you aspire to more, you can do so, here in America. That, sir, is a blessing I can and will repay."

Brympton did not answer at first. Harry was content to gather his thoughts and emotions. He worried that his voice had been too shrill. He did not intend to leave for basic training under a cloud.

Brympton cleared his throat. The sound was wet with congestion. "Harry, you are meant to make a noise in the world, and that noise is not the thud of a cannon or the bark of a rifle." He paused to cough. "You've been teaching students at the college ever since you graduated. You did more good at Muskingum College than you could possibly do in that wretched war. You are that most dangerous thing—an idealist. I fear you believe the nonsense they spout. A war to end all wars? Mankind will *never* be rid of war. As long as men envy and steal what they cannot create, there will be war." His hand slipped from the blanket again and he pointed a slender finger at Harry. "I fear that they will grind your bones for meal."

"And I fear you'll go to your reward while I'm away," Harry blurted.

They both fell silent again.

A robin hopped across the yard thirty feet from Brympton's chair, digging into the cold ground with its beak. Brympton studied the bird for a while, and then said, "They lay their eggs this month. If they've had enough to eat."

"I saw a nest in the eaves on the south side of the manor," Harry said.

"The eaves haven't been cared for properly since your father passed away."

"I should have done that for you."

"Nonsense," Brympton said. "The fault is mine. I've given the servants reason to believe that any sort of slipshod work will do." He took a ragged breath. "I tire too easily. That is my excuse."

Harry shifted in his chair, facing Brympton. "I'll make a deal with you, sir. I promise to survive this war if you promise to be here when I return."

"More stuff and nonsense," Brympton said. "But I'll accept your deal and depend on you to keep your end."

Harry smiled gratefully. Sitting back, he watched the robin worry at the cold ground until it gave up and flew off.

•   •   •

France, 1918

For Harry, who had never traveled outside of Ohio, the world seemed astoundingly large as seen from train and ship windows. When he was younger, he'd gauged everything by the distance between New Concord and the graveyard where his parents lay resting. Now, the world included a moving panorama, studied through a window to the clacking of rails and the rocking of waves.

That same world shrank again, as if he'd gazed into the wrong end of a telescope once he reached the front. Instead of open skies and fields, Harry's world consisted of fortified dirt walls and duckboard paths, sandbags, and lice.

Rats were his constant companions. Harry quickly developed a fear of rodents, while for their part, they seemed to be less and less concerned by his presence. How was he supposed to rest when those filthy vermin might steal food from his pockets or nip his sleeping face?

Harry's platoon was sent to bolster the French lines under the command of a French officer—Captain Martin. After stand-to each morning, the captain marched from one end of his command to the other, with a friendly nod to his countrymen and a harsh word for the Americans. "He thinks we're all lazy," Drew said. "He sleeps in a dugout with a cot and a lantern and wonders why we aren't buttoned up." He paused. "Except for *you*, Harry. You're a picture, aren't you?"

Harry ignored him, gazing down the line. A quick burst of activity gave away the captain's approach. "Martin is coming."

Drew stood up and put on his helmet.

"Captain," Harry said, snapping to attention. Drew followed—a half beat behind.

Captain Martin paused to frown. "Why aren't you men repairing the trench?" he demanded.

Drew pointed at the section that they'd just finished shoring up. "We did, sir."

Captain Martin scowled. "So, this is the only five feet of trench in all of Europe?"

There was no point in answering.

Captain Martin touched his perfect mustache and pointed at Drew. "Your uniform is a disgrace. Your name?"

"Private Drew Peterson."

Captain Martin turned to Harry and then back to Drew. "You would do well to model this man, Private Peterson. At least he knows how to *look* like a soldier."

When the captain moved on, Drew gave Harry an angry glance. "He's a bastard."

Harry nodded. "Martin is a martinet."

"A marionette."

Harry laughed. "Your best yet."

Drew took off his helmet and sat down. "The French officers are buffoons." The whistle of artillery had begun again, but Harry wasn't worried. The whistle was only audible after the shell passed over the trench. A long whistle meant a shell that would land far, far beyond. Drew shifted, trying to get comfortable. "Did they have anything to say about your idea?"

Harry had proposed setting up wireless telegraph communication between the trenches and command. Captain Martin had listened to him without interruption, thanked Harry, and promised to advance the idea. That had been weeks earlier. "I don't expect them to."

"Such a waste," Drew said. "You are a genius. You could be doing things to end this war. Instead, you're mucking around in the trench with the rest of us."

Harry shrugged helplessly.

"I would be happier if you'd get angry, Harry."

"There's no point."

Drew leaned back against the log wall and closed his eyes. "You should stand up for yourself. This is like the car ignition, all over again." Drew was outraged to discover that the invention of electric automobile ignitions had been credited to some General Motors engineers—Coleman and Kettering. "You invented electrical ignition, and no one knows it. Now every car and truck uses your invention, and you won't see a penny of the profit."

Harry sat down carefully. It had rained the night before, and some spots on the duckboard were wet and muddy. "When something is ready to be invented or discovered," Harry said, "it's likely that several men are working on the problem. My interest is in solving problems. I don't spend a lot of time worrying about credit."

"That's why you need me to be your manager," Drew said.

Harry laughed. "Yes, yes. You'll do your *Drew diligence*, and we'll all be rich."

"Filthy rich."

Harry looked around him. "Halfway there," he whispered. The trench was littered with shards of wood, bits of cloth, wrappers, rat droppings, shell casings, wire, a sheet of corrugated steel, straw, and wood planking. He wiped at his mouth with his fingertips.

Drew looked skyward as a whistling sound announced another errant shell. "I wish I were home."

"I know."

"So, why do you tolerate that bastard captain of ours?"

Harry shook his head, disgusted. "I don't think any more of him than you. We feel the same about him."

"Then why—"

"*Because to hell with him, that's why.*"

Drew tilted his head back against the trench wall, his eyes wide with surprise. "You cursed. I've never heard you curse before."

Harry tried to smile. "You're to blame. You keep poking a finger in my wound." He breathed in, trying to slow his heart. He would never admit as much, but here in the trenches, his nerves would have gotten the better of him had Drew not been by his side. Even with Drew's presence, the lack of sleep, the constant threat of attack, and the endless shelling had taken its toll. Wasn't it the same for every man here?

"As for our captain," Harry continued, "I detest the man. He thinks we are all dime novel cowboys. I won't give him the satisfaction of validating his poor judgement."

Drew nodded with enthusiasm.

Harry continued. "The French are so very pompous. With the Russian front settled, the only thing saving the French and English from the Germans are the Americans, and they don't dare acknowledge it."

Drew smirked. "Good thing you've no interest in receiving proper credit."

Harry's turn to laugh. He grabbed a clod of dirt from the duckboard and pitched it at Drew halfheartedly. "Now *I* wish you were home."

A shot in the distance announced a sniper. Nothing close enough to worry over. But between shells and sniper fire, the Germans might be working their way up to some sort of night operation. The thought of another night without sleep made Harry's stomach turn.

Drew sighed. "I wish, I wish I could be with her." Drew had married his longtime girlfriend, Margaret after graduating college. They'd been happy. Harry knew Drew missed her terribly.

Barking came from the east.

"Terriers," Harry said. "I hope they catch some rats."

Drew ignored him. "I never told you," he said.

"Told me what?"

Drew grimaced. "I'll tell you because it eats at me. But you must promise never to bring the subject up again." Then, he was silent.

Harry waited. If Drew chose to continue, he would do so. Otherwise, the false start would slip away easily enough.

At last, Drew said, "I did not give her a proper farewell. She wanted . . . to be close that last night. But I was too excited. Ready to save the world. My mind was already on the train."

Harry nodded without comment.

"Since we shipped out, her letters have been . . . reserved," Drew finished.

"There are other obvious explanations," Harry said. "For example, have you told her what the trenches are like? Have you told her about the rats?"

"Of course not," Drew said, frowning. "There are things I will *never* tell her."

"Then your letters to her are *reserved*." Drew sat still, listening. "Perhaps she misses you terribly, and doesn't want to burden you with that. That seems much more plausible than her holding some sort of grudge. She loves you, man. Don't be an idiot." Harry glanced to his right.

"We should offer the other fellows a hand. Like Captain Marionette suggested."

Drew exhaled. "You should be inventing something instead of digging. That is the real disgrace."

"I didn't invent wireless telegraph. I offered to construct what has already been invented. With improvements, of course."

"You could invent a weapon, then."

"No," Harry said, his voice guttural.

"You should put that giant brain of yours to work on solving the problem of war."

"War is not a problem."

Drew gestured to their dirt and log home, a look of disbelief on his face. "This is not a problem?" He stood up, brushing off his seat, helmet in hand. His blond curls were pasted to his head with sweat and dirt.

"I mean that war is part of the human condition," Harry said. As he stood, he thought of his conversation with Brympton in the garden. "That condition cannot change. It resides, cell deep. Mr. Brympton said as much before you and I left for basic." He paused. "Death is much the same. Death cannot be *solved*. Everyone dies."

"That's cheerful."

Harry shrugged. "Killing people fast and efficiently? *That's* a problem—one I won't spend a single moment trying to solve. I'll leave that to others. In a way, I'm being used exactly as I would wish when I dig trenches or lay planks. Better that than—"

There was no warning sound—just an intense light that blinded him. Harry was dimly aware he'd been pitched back against the trench wall, bashing his head against the logs. Stunned, he tried to focus and couldn't. His ears were plugged, as if they'd been packed with wax. He tried to move his right arm, but it was pinned underneath him. He tried his left arm next and was able to touch his face. His fingers came away wet. He reached down and touched his groin. No apparent damage.

Still half-blind, he struggled to a sitting position. His right arm dangled uselessly at his side, surely broken. He called out to Drew but couldn't hear his own voice.

A German shell had landed nearby. How close? He could not tell. In the distance, he could hear shouts. Turning to his right, he saw someone leaning in close, his mouth moving. *Not so distant, then.* His ears must have been damaged. He did not want to be deaf.

Or blind. He fixed his gaze on the soldier shouting at him, and gradually, he was able to focus. He turned back to Drew but could not locate him. He glanced down at his blood-covered uniform. "Drew?" He could barely make out his words. "Drew?"

The soldier to his right was batting at Harry's right thigh with a piece of someone's shirt. His leg was on fire, though he couldn't feel a thing. He imagined he would soon enough. He turned back again, spotting a boot. Drew's boot.

A foot still in the boot.

He turned to his left. There, embedded in the trench wall, was a fragment of skull, covered in bloody flesh and dirty blond hair. He grabbed for the fragment. Drew was dead. Dead. The shell had blown him to pieces. How was Harry still alive? Had his friend shielded him from the worst of the blast?

He looked down again. So much blood! Drew's blood.

Another soldier tried to pry the piece of skull from his fingers. "No!" Harry growled. "Don't touch me! Don't touch me!" He wrested the skull cap away from the man and tucked it under his right armpit, shielding it with his dangling arm. They were going to send more than tags home to New Concord. Drew's parents deserved—

Then, the pain hit him. It continued, long after the medic arrived with a morphine syringe.

· · · · ·

November 30, 1918

Dear Sir,

It is with deep regret that I write to inform you that Elias Brympton passed away on the 17th day of November from a prolonged illness. I had occasion to speak with him when news of the war's end reached New Concord. He was as happy as I've seen him and I know that he looked forward to your return.

As his friend and advisor, we had many occasions to discuss your finer qualities—aspects of character, I would add, that mirrored Elias's own.

As his lawyer, I prepared his amended last will and testament. It will come as no surprise that he left the manor and its grounds to the college he so faithfully served, as well as many of his other investments. However, he made a generous provision for you. I understand that you are still in hospital. When you return to New Concord, we can make the necessary arrangements.

As Elias had no children of his own, I believe he regarded you as a son. His provision will make you a wealthy man. I know that he wished you to be able to pursue whatever projects you desired, and within reason, that wish will be fulfilled.

This letter's news will almost certainly darken the triumph that you and your fellow soldiers have so richly earned. Know that he was proud of you, and that his final thoughts were likely of you.

Yours sincerely,
Jonathan Bennington
Attorney at Law

CHAPTER SIX

A Simple Matter/The Applicant

Ohio, 1920

Making dinner should have been a simple matter. First, he would walk into New Concord, stopping at the baker, the butcher, and Mrs. Hartley's cottage. Next, he would cook the meal and eat. He'd wrap the leftover bread for breakfast the following morning and then clean up. Simple.

Harry spent the morning in his laboratory, working on altered versions of the coil antenna. He wondered briefly if any new correspondence had arrived from his research friends but didn't think he'd have time to visit the post office. Time was forever in short supply. In fact, at the very moment he dismissed the possibility of collecting his mail, he noticed the angle of the sun, and realized it was setting. Where had time gone? Had he been so focused that he'd let the day escape him?

He grabbed a coat and headed for town, kicking dirt as he walked. There had been progress with the coil. Now, that would have to wait. Eating was such a burden! A resented intrusion. He tried to keep a quick pace, though the scars on his leg restricted his motion, and his leg throbbed like the electric cure.

At the bakery, Mr. Albanesi saw him and held the door, ushering him inside. "Professor! You honor me with your presence! What can I give you this fine day?" The glass case against the far wall was mostly empty, though Harry spotted a pair of rolls that might suit his purpose.

Albanesi would not hear of it. "I have something special for you! A rosemary and garlic loaf. My wife grew the herbs in her garden, special for you."

Rosemary. Garlic. The leftovers would not be right for breakfast. "That sounds wonderful," Harry said. "Adventurous."

Mr. Albanesi blushed and patted the strands of hair that rested on his head like tie-down ropes on a flatbed. "You'll see. This will be your favorite." He slipped sideways, graceful for a man so round, and stood in front of the cash register. His face grew suddenly serious. "Let me give you this loaf. Just this once."

"No," Harry said. "I wouldn't think of it. This being a special loaf—"

Jovial again, Albanesi laughed. "This is why I make a loaf just for you. You won't accept a gift, so I make the loaf special and charge you the normal price. That is my trick." He winked as he wrapped the loaf in brown paper. Hair covered his arms—far more than what covered his head. "Ten cents, then."

Harry placed the dime on top of the glass case. "Worth every penny."

"Yes, you'll see!" Albanesi said. "Would you like something to drink?"

"No, thank you," Harry said. "I fear I'm behind my time." And he was. The butcher shop was closed when he arrived. Luckily, the butcher's wife, Mrs. Campbell, spotted him through the window and unlocked the door.

"Thank you so much," he said. "I've inconvenienced you."

"Not at all," she said, bustling behind the counter. "It's the very least I can do for a war hero."

Harry winced.

In just a few minutes, he was on his way again, the loaf of bread and a thick pork chop wrapped in paper and tucked under his arm. The sun was setting, but he had one more stop. The recently widowed Mrs. Hartley kept chickens at her cottage, and he needed an egg. Maybe two.

Mrs. Hartley greeted him at the door. Harry suspected that she spent her evenings perched in front of her window, surveying the fringes of New Concord. The russet sky might have otherwise hidden his approach. "Professor!" she said, her voice ripe with enthusiasm. "What a wonderful surprise!"

"I seem to be quite late for a visit," Harry said, tugging at his overcoat. The night air had turned. "I hoped to prevail upon you for an egg or two for my dinner."

"Oh!" she said, clasping her hands across her bosom. "I have soup on the stove, and I've made far too much for one old woman. Would you come in and share a late supper with me?" Her eyelids fluttered in a disturbing way, and though the cottage looked warm and inviting, Harry demurred. "Thank you so much, but another time," Harry said. He pulled out the brown wrapper containing the pork chop and held it out. "I've a pork chop here and must return to finish my work."

"Always working," Mrs. Hartley scolded.

"*Idle hands are the devil's tools*," Harry said, quoting Chaucer.

"*One monster there is in the world*," she said. "*The idle man.*"

Harry tilted his head in surprise. "Thomas Carlyle! A secret pleasure of mine. Mrs. Hartley, you amaze me."

She blushed and waved him off. "My mother and father were Scots, you know. What did you expect? Eggs then. No stew?"

"No stew, thank you."

She stepped into the night and scuttled off to the chicken coop, humming as she went. Harry waited patiently, passing the time by gazing at the night sky. His old friend the moon showed him her one side, cut by shadow into an arc, like the blade of a scythe. The reaper's scythe, he decided. Alone in the yard, the last vestiges of autumn—crushed leaves, bonfire smoke, and the soft glow of plum-colored sky—left him feeling melancholy. He thought of his best friend Drew, his beloved Mr. Brympton, and his mother and father. As Mrs. Hartley made her way back to him, eggs nestled in her apron, he was surprised to discover that his cheeks were wet. He'd been weeping. He wiped his face with his coat sleeve and stepped into the shadows so as not to give himself away.

"I find I've come here without a sack," he said, forcing an even tone.

"I have a sack for you, Professor."

"I'm quite a bother—"

"No bother at all!" She hurried into the cottage and returned with a small paper sack filled with four eggs. "I've given you four so that you can have a proper breakfast in the morning. You are too thin, Professor. Winter's on the doorstep, and that threadbare coat will do you no good."

"I'm fine, really."

Her eyebrows turned down, and he prepared himself for a lecture. "You need someone to take care of you, Professor. Men run the world, so they've no time for the details of daily life."

He stared at her rosy cheeks, glowing in the light coming from the open cottage door. "You are too kind. What do I owe you?"

"Your company?" she asked. "Come for dinner next week and we'll be even."

"A bargain," he said. He hated to lie, but this wasn't the first time. He would not come to dinner. He would not give her the wrong impression.

Mr. Hartley had passed beyond life just three months earlier, victim to the great influenza epidemic. She'd nursed him with Epsom salts and castor oil, but when he began bleeding from the nose and ears, she'd known the outcome, and arranged for a plot in the New Concord cemetery. In the end, pneumonia took him, and he was carried away by neighbors. Mrs. Hartley grieved for a week or more, and then seemed to rebound, more cheerful than before. Mr. Hartley had been a dour man, and his absence seemed to unleash a new enthusiasm for life that found its expression in her appetite for food. She was not a small woman.

Harry thanked her and insisted that she close and lock the door before he would leave. Once she was gone, he put a quarter on the step and walked to the road.

The last part of his journey sapped his remaining energy. He considered forgoing his supper. But he'd already taken pains, and he was hungry. He wondered if Mrs. Hartley would be insulted by his payment. Perhaps he should not have left the quarter, though she was a widow and surely needed money. On the other hand, he did not want to hurt her feelings. A quarter had no purchasing power in the realm of self-esteem.

Finally home, he heated the enameled gas stove and melted some bacon fat in a cast iron skillet, just as he'd done as a child. Then, he broke one egg and whipped it in a bowl. He dredged the pork chop in flour, then egg, and then flour again. Into the pan.

When the chop was cooked, he took the bread loaf and meat to the table. Sitting down, he felt the last of his energy seep through his legs, as if he were a barrel with a hole in the bottom. He sat, hands in his lap, considering the pork chop. He'd meant to season the flour, but he'd forgotten. He wished, momentarily, for a glass of wine, but Prohibition made such things difficult. Mrs. Hartley probably had some schnapps set aside. He might have asked. But she'd have insisted that they share a drink, and that was not anything he could allow.

Plump as pudding, she was also forty-eight years old. He was twenty-eight, though when fully considering the matter, he felt *much* older than her. She believed in love and happiness, fat chickens, and good advice.

Harry believed in nothing beyond his research. The rest was pain.

·　　·　　·　　·　　·

The cottage was a charming affair with a wood plank exterior, painted gray, and a tiny, picturesque windmill on the roof. No front porch. Perhaps there was a porch in the rear. Elizabeth Rose paused at the professor's door. She touched her hair lightly, then brushed the front of her dress. Everything in its place. She must knock, or she must leave. To stand still would be absurd.

She knocked.

No answer. Was he home? She'd walked from her parents' house on the far side of New Concord. She leaned forward to knock again, but the door opened. She stepped back and smiled.

The man at the door smiled back. "Yes?"

"Hello," she said. "My name is Elizabeth Rose. Betty Hartley sent me—"

"Betty?" The man seemed confused.

"The widow Hartley."

"Ah. Mrs. Hartley." The man smiled again. Soft brown eyes, long lashes. Just as she'd remembered.

"Mrs. Hartley mentioned, quite in passing, that you might require the assistance of a housekeeper. I am here to offer my services."

"I'm sorry. I'm a little confused. Has someone placed an advert?"

"No," Elizabeth said. She could feel herself blush. "Mrs. Hartley suggested that the lack of a housekeeper might be hindering your research. I am currently looking for a position, and I thought that our situations might be mutually beneficial."

The professor stepped out onto his tiny front porch and pulled the door shut behind him. He was a slender man with a pale complexion. His eyes were his most striking feature—kind and bright. "I am sorry to disappoint you—"

She forged ahead. "I am a good cook. I launder and mend clothing. I will keep your home clean and dusted, polish your silver—"

"I don't have silver," he said. "I recently purchased a steel alternative that purports to be stainless, though my experience tells me otherwise."

Elizabeth Rose stood silent. There seemed to be nothing to say.

"Do you have references?"

She nodded, pulling her shoulder bag open. The bag was hand-tooled leather—among her belongings, a sole extravagance. Her dress and shoes were plain. She'd seen the bag in a shop window and saved the two dollars over a period of weeks, often returning to the store in fear that the bag had been sold. She pulled a folded sheet of paper from inside the otherwise empty bag and handed it over.

The professor unfolded the letter and scanned the contents. "Was this your only domestic job?"

She swallowed. "Yes, sir. I have been in the workforce for a limited time. The job was temporary." She nodded at the letter of recommendation. "But I do good work."

He shrugged and handed the paper back. "I'm not sure I can afford you."

She frowned. Everyone knew that the professor was a man of means. "I ask a reasonable wage—nothing more." Her gaze focused on his slender frame. "To my eye, sir, you seem to need a cook at the very least."

"Oh?" He seemed amused.

"I am very good with the cheapest cuts of meat. They are often the most flavorful cuts, but they need to be prepared properly. You may find that hiring me saves you money."

He leaned against the door, one eyebrow raised and a turn of the mouth that was more of a spasm than a smile.

A misstep. She tried not to panic. She *needed* this job. She could not stay with her parents another winter. "Save you money on food, I mean. Food." She took a deep breath. "Your real savings will be time, sir. I'm told that you're an inventor. I can provide you with time at a minimal cost."

His smile softened. "*That* is a good argument." But he stayed in place, resting his thin frame against the door.

She was certain he did not recognize her. Why would he? She'd been his student at the college four long years ago. Since he did not remember her, she had no intention of trying to trade on their past acquaintance. "Well, then. What say you?"

"Tell me again how you came here. You say that Mrs. Hartley sent you?"

Elizabeth tried for a casual tone. "She seems very concerned about your well-being."

"Yes. She's a generous soul." He looked thoughtful. She might have expected him to say something else about the widow, something derogatory, and was glad that he didn't. He stood straight, pushing away from the door. "Let's discuss wages," he said.

Having agreed on a figure, he opened the door and showed her inside. "I live with minimal belongings," he said. "A Spartan life appeals to me. But you may have additional needs. If you require something for your work, I will provide it."

The professor's cottage consisted of a front room, small kitchen, and three more back rooms. Standing in the doorway, she could see much of the house. A plain table and chairs looked sturdy and comfortable. An oval rug sat in the center of the front room near the fireplace, though with little else around it, the rug looked lonely and forlorn. The mantel over the fireplace was bare.

The one surprising feature was an upright piano. Though tall and plain, without ornamentation, fine craftsmanship was evident in the trim lines and immaculate woodwork. "How wonderful," she said. "You play, then?"

"No," he answered. His tone led her to believe that the subject was not open for discussion.

On the far side of the room, a door was open, revealing an unmade bed and nothing else. As she moved across the wooden floors onto the oval rug, she saw that the back room to the left was empty, save for a few boxes. The door to the room on the right was closed.

"That room stays closed," he said. "You may busy yourself anywhere in the house but there." She waited for a further explanation, but none came. She surmised that the room contained his workshop.

"Do you have running water?" she asked. The cottage was situated on the outskirts of New Concord and seemed very old. Not what she was expecting at all.

"Yes, in the kitchen," he said. "The bathroom as well." He pointed at the bedroom. "Through the door and to the left. So, what do you think?"

"You are all economy, sir."

"Yes," he said, sniffing. "I suppose you'll want to put a flower vase somewhere."

She laughed. The sound echoed, startling her. "Why yes, I suppose I will." She turned to look at him. He seemed to be staring at the empty wall across the room—there were no pictures hanging anywhere—and she wondered what he was thinking. There was no way of telling.

When she'd taken a class in the sciences from the professor, he'd been warm and engaging, interacting with his students rather than lecturing them from afar. He was not a podium professor. Now? He'd listened to her attentively enough. He was all politeness. But standing on his oval rug, she had the distinct impression that he was as alone as if she were gone from the room entirely.

CHAPTER SEVEN

A Narrow Escape/That Which is Not Stew

Ohio, 1920

The professor introduced his new housekeeper to the few vendors in town with whom he had accounts—the baker, the butcher, and most importantly, the hardware salesman. He arranged for Elizabeth to pick up his mail at the post office. On the way back, he stopped at Mrs. Hartley's to give thanks for recommending Elizabeth's employment. Though she was distant at first, his heartfelt gratitude warmed her, and she began dispensing other bits of advice and wisdom, from fashion ("Your coat is not just worn, it's out of date") to matters of the heart ("A man living alone will die a decade too soon").

Elizabeth waited without speaking, her hands folded. The Hartley family had been friendly with her parents for as long as she could remember, and when she visited to pay her respects, Mrs. Hartley always seemed warm and inviting. But today, the old woman barely looked her way.

After a polite interval, the professor appeared to be trying to disengage himself. Mrs. Hartley managed to link her arm with his, holding him fast. She was a short woman, and when she pulled him close, like reeling in a fish, she gazed directly into his chest. "Come inside, come inside," she said. She cast a glance back at Elizabeth, a cryptic smile on her face. "Come along," she ordered, as if speaking to a child.

Inside, Mrs. Hartley released him to a chair and busied herself making tea, chattering all the while. Finally seated at her table, a kettle and teacups readied, she stopped, looked him head-on, and said, "Tell me about your experiences in the war." Not a question, but a demand.

"The subject is too distasteful for such fine company."

"Nonsense," Mrs. Hartley assured him. "I nursed Mr. Hartley until the end, him bathed in blood and whatnot. I'm a woman of the world." She turned to Elizabeth, giving her a sympathetic nod. "You might not want to hear these things. But it's important for our men to be able to express themselves. If you wanted to take a walk outside—"

"No, I'm fine, thank you."

Harry, on the other hand, did not look fine. His face had gone pale, and his eyes had a hollow, vacant look.

Mrs. Hartley took his hand. "So, tell me about war."

"I'd prefer not."

"Nonsense," she said again. "I insist."

"People die." The words had a chiseled finality. His voice had gone dark. His lower jaw began moving side to side as if he were grinding his teeth.

Mrs. Hartley continued, offering a stream of assurances coupled with more questions. Did someone he know die? How many Germans did he kill? Did it hurt to be wounded? At length, she again suggested that Elizabeth take a walk. "Perhaps the professor will feel more at ease, dear."

"I'm certain that you're right," Elizabeth said. She turned to the professor, saying, "But I must remind you of our appointment with the lawyer."

He gazed at her, a blank expression on his face. "Lawyer," he repeated.

"The matter of your accounts." Elizabeth's face felt hot. *I am not a good liar*, she thought.

He stood up, spilling some of his untouched tea. "I wish that you'd reminded me earlier," he said, his voice thick with apparent frustration. He turned to Mrs. Hartley and bowed. "My apologies, madame. I am behind my time. Thank you again for your help and support." He turned to Elizabeth, glaring. "Shall we proceed?"

Mrs. Hartley followed them to the door, sputtering as she went, but he was outside before further discussion could continue. Elizabeth followed, mystified. He seemed genuinely angry with her. Did he have an actual appointment with his lawyer? He hurried to the road and turned away from town, as if to return home. She scurried after him, catching up in time to catch the hint of a smile on his face.

The sky was as cold and white as the inside of an icebox. Winter would soon make its appearance. Once snow began to fall, the walk from her parents' house to the professor's cottage would be difficult. The dogwoods, chinkapin oaks, and sweetgums along their path were nearly bare. Only the occasional shortleaf pine looked ready to weather the coming season. Winters did not last long in New Concord, but they could be bitterly cold.

The professor walked on without saying anything. The silence worried her, so she tried to explain herself. "My parents have been friends with the Hartleys since before Mr. Hartley died. Mrs. Hartley means well, but . . ." She wanted to say something kind, but nothing came to mind.

"She's lonely," he said. His voice was soft, and the cold air almost carried it away. "Everyone has faults, and everyone has needs. Sometimes, the needs are so great that the faults overwhelm one's sensibilities."

Elizabeth thought about this before saying, "You have a generous outlook."

Harry waved her comment away. "You saved me. I am at a loss in the face of certain situations. I saw no way to extricate myself."

"I thought you were genuinely angry with me."

"Not in the least," Harry said. His face gave no hint to his thoughts.

The road was badly rutted, showing the effects of the recent rains. She kept her gaze on her plain brown shoes, with the voice of her mother ringing in her ears—"Watch your step, you stupid, stupid girl. If you fall, it will be your own fault."

Harry interrupted her thoughts. "I suppose I was angry with myself. Social situations are like a battlefield, mined and wired. I am unable to cross over." He shook his head. "The piano," he added. Then he was silent, as if those two words explained everything.

"The piano," she repeated.

"Edison is widely regarded as a genius. I think that his real talent lies in his focus. The man never sleeps." He walked on, hands in the pockets of his waistcoat. His long stride forced her to move as quickly as she dared. "Edison's work pattern has been an inspiration. I follow his lead. By narrowing my fields of interest, I have more time to devote to my projects." He was silent again for nearly a quarter mile.

"And the piano?" she ventured.

He glanced at her as if he'd forgotten she was there. "The piano? Ah." He nodded. "Had I taken a different path, I might have been a musician."

She could see the professor's cottage in the distance.

"When I returned from Europe, I received a generous endowment from Professor Brympton of Muskingum College. I was frugal with the funds—"

"Spartan," she said.

He glanced her way, the corners of his mouth twitching. "Yes, Spartan. As I was saying, Edison is successful because of his focus. I pursue a similar focus. When I was a young boy, Professor Brympton advised me to do just that. He was a great influence in my life." He stopped. "I was raised on the Brympton estate. Perhaps I didn't explain that."

"I didn't know," she said.

"Focusing on one field of endeavor limits one's efforts in another." He reached the flagstone path that led to the front door of his cottage. "When I received my endowment, I allowed myself a single indulgence. The piano is a promise to myself. It will be my reward for the hard work that will yield a happy and prosperous future." He said this last phrase in a flat voice. Whether from the wind or from some inner turmoil, his eyes were dark and misty.

"I could teach you to play," she offered.

He shook his head. "That would squander the time I've purchased by hiring you." He walked across his small yard, careful to step on flagstones rather than the mud that remained from the storms. Elizabeth hurried after him, almost slipping.

"I will play for you, then," she called.

He turned at the door and met her gaze, head tilted. "I would enjoy that."

"Thank you for telling me about your piano."

"Thank you for rescuing me from the widow Hartley," he answered. Once inside, he entered his workshop, closing the door behind him.

•   •   •   •   •

The meat they'd bought from the butcher was stringy. Clearly, the professor intended to test her boast about cooking with cheap cuts. She checked the cupboard for ingredients and decided on a beef stew. Cold weather food, for certain. She lined the bottom of a pan with thickly sliced onion and carrot, followed by a layer of meat cut into tiny pieces. She added salt, pepper, and then a layer of canned green beans, chopped into bite-sized pieces. Last, she cut up a potato and topped the concoction. The liquid from the canned beans would be enough to make a rich stew. She topped the pan with a heavy lid and made a note of the time. Two hours should suffice.

The cottage itself was tidy in the way that empty, unused places avoided clutter. Elizabeth imagined that the professor spent almost all of his time in the workshop. That room was probably a mess, but not one she needed to worry about. She wasted little time dusting and sweeping. Clothes and bedding needed washing, but she'd made considerable headway by the time the stew was ready.

A poorly wrapped half-loaf of bread was still good—*waste not, want not.* The loaf smelled of rosemary. *Excellent.* She'd have wanted some herbs to add to the stew, and the cupboard had nothing to offer. With winter coming, Harry Browning had precious little in the way of canned goods. When spring came, she would plant a garden. Until then, she would depend on goods from town.

Taking the loaf to the sink, she cut off the stale end and then sectioned the remainder so that he could dip the bread in his stew. Outside, the sun hung low in the sky. The professor was still working, and she did not want his supper to grow cold. She set the table, laying out a fork and spoon with a glass of water. She couldn't find any cloth napkins and made a note to bring one or two from home. She would fill his bowl when he was done working.

Another hour passed. It would be dark soon, and she worried about her walk home. She'd hoped he'd enjoy the food and congratulate himself on a clever hire. As it was, she'd need to add water to the stew to reheat it. She readied the oil lamp and sat at the table, drumming her fingers.

By the time the sun set, she was in full panic. She placed the stew over a flame, telling herself that by the time supper was once again hot, the professor would have emerged from the workshop. When he did not appear, she filled a bowl, put it on the table, and crossed over to the closed door. Steeling herself, she knocked.

No answer.

She knocked again, louder this time, and the door flew open. He looked disheveled and a little angry. "Yes?"

Elizabeth stepped back. "Your supper is on the table."

He blinked once. "The point of hiring you was to give myself time for uninterrupted work."

Elizabeth felt her cheeks flush hot. "I am most sorry to inconvenience you," she said, her voice clipped as if she were talking to her very own father. "It is past dark, and you have not eaten."

He blinked again—once, twice. He gazed out the window, and then looked back down at Elizabeth. "So it is," he said, pulling the door closed behind him. "I do not have a window in my workshop, and it seems that time has escaped me." He sniffed the air. "What have you prepared?"

"Beef stew," she said, trying to keep her voice level.

"Stew," he repeated. He went to the table and looked down at the bowl. "This is mine?" he asked.

Use your noodle, she thought. *You are the only one here.*

He sat down, stared at the bowl, then the sliced bread, and finally the flatware. He took up the spoon and tasted the stew. Tilting his head, he licked his lips and made a humming sound. Another spoonful. He sat back and met her gaze.

"I don't like stew," he said.

Elizabeth's heart sank. "I didn't—"

"However, I like this very much." He gave her an odd smile. "Therefore, it can't be stew."

"It is stew, sir. I've been—"

"My logic is infallible. I don't like stew. I like this. Therefore, this can't be stew." He beamed, apparently quite pleased with his jest.

Her cheeks burned again. "Your statement is logical but invalid. And your opinion of my cooking, good or bad, is neither a necessary—nor a sufficient—criteria for any known definition of stew."

Harry dropped his spoon. It clattered on the table.

My God. One day on the job and I've lost my position.

He turned his head slightly, though his gaze did not leave her. "There is much more to you than meets the eye," he said. He retrieved the spoon and began eating again, pausing only to dip bread into the bowl. He ate as if he'd not had a meal in days. In the matter of two minutes, he'd wiped the bowl clean. Looking up, he asked, "Did you eat?"

"No s-sir," she stammered. *Where is the professor I remember? This man is full of applesauce.*

"Well, you should set a place for two when you cook."

That surprised her. Clearly, the professor did not put much stock in convention. "Perhaps next time." She glanced out the window. Dark as the tomb outside. "I will put aside the leftovers. You've no icebox, but I can cover the pan and put it outside. The lid is heavy. Nothing without hands will get inside of it."

"Leave it. I'll have more later." Her expression must have given her away because he followed with, "I really *did* like it. Best meal I've had in weeks."

"I'm glad," she said, but her voice lacked enthusiasm. She was suddenly very tired. The walk home would be arduous. She grabbed her coat—as threadbare as his own—and walked to the door. As soon as she turned the knob, a gust of icy wind blew the door wide open.

"Good God," he said. "The wind is not our friend. We should have set off much earlier."

"You didn't want to be interrupted."

His shoulders sagged. "That was quite rude of me. Forgive me, please. I am used to living alone. It has made a barbarian of me."

"No need to apologize," she said, thinking that he very well did need to apologize and be as gallant as possible while doing so.

He walked to the door and peered outside. "This is not good."

She silently agreed.

"Well then," he said, his voice suddenly cheery. "Time for an evening walk."

"That isn't necessary—"

"Or sufficient? Not sufficient, perhaps. I have amends to make. But necessary? Absolutely." He went for his coat, returning with a lantern in hand. "Let's be off, shall we?"

Once on the path, she said, "You can't walk me home every night."

"We'll see," he told her.

CHAPTER EIGHT

A Rose by Any Other Name/Interlude/Thorns

Ohio, 1920

Having delivered her safely home, the professor turned back, head down and shoulders hunched against the wind. When he was out of sight, Elizabeth Rose stepped inside the cottage to face her parents.

Rutherford Rose, named by his mother for the president of the United States, more closely resembled William Howard Taft. Three full inches under six feet, Rutherford weighed nearly three hundred pounds. Though he ate a great deal, keeping the family pantry forever empty, the real secret to his girth was his ability to avoid exertion. He had no real profession. He labored during the spring and at harvest time on neighboring farms—often working half-days, owing to various physical maladies. His employers were generous to a fault, for they paid him in full and rehired him for every planting and harvest.

By contrast, Constance Rose was a human spindle. Her face, rumored to have been pretty once, played a single, bitter theme. Frown lines, deep and permanent, echoed throughout her face in squints and wrinkles. She added to the meager family income through endless needlework, spending every day hunched over her sewing. When she and her husband argued, she brandished her needles like weapons. Elizabeth imagined she would one day find her father dead, stuck like a pincushion, for there was no doubt that if her parents' arguments ever came to blows, her mother would win.

Neighbors were frequently generous, and Rutherford was eager to accept whatever came his way, especially the food. Constance made no comment, never offering thanks for any gift. Instead, she sat silent, needles darting, with a sour, judgmental look on her face. Others lived blessed lives, and small acts of charity were a sorry substitute for life in an unfair world.

The kindness of others continued though, owing much to Elizabeth herself. Her good nature was a constant source of surprise, given what was known of her parents.

Under normal circumstances, Elizabeth could never have attended Muskingum College, despite her quick mind. Muskingum was one of the early coeducational colleges, so she was technically eligible for enrollment. Her parents, however, were working poor—in her father's case, the barely working poor. A degree from Muskingum was far beyond their means.

Elizabeth had imagined a plain future for herself. Perhaps she could marry. She was an attractive girl. Any conquest would need to overlook her family, though.

Then fate—in the guise of Professor Elias Brympton— intervened. One of Elizabeth's teachers in the public school was acquainted with the good professor, and championed her cause. After a brief interview, wherein Elizabeth discussed the natural sciences with Professor Brympton, Elizabeth found herself sponsored for a college education.

Her parents were bitterly opposed to the arrangement. "Why doesn't he simply give you a lump sum and let you decide how best to spend it?" her father demanded.

"What does this personage expect from you in return?" her mother wondered. "It's a scandal, to be sure."

Elizabeth ignored their criticisms. An education meant a future, and she had no intention of letting her parents squander her one chance. Because she'd always suffered their indignities in silence, they were surprised to find her so intractable. "I wonder if you're a changeling," her mother said. "That would explain your ingratitude." She put her needles down and regarded her daughter, eyes narrowed to slits. "You're not as smart as you think you are. Not by half."

Smart enough to leave this place, Elizabeth thought.

Tonight, both her parents were awake, sitting in the dim light of the ramshackle cottage. Her mother had put aside her sewing for the evening, a sure sign of the late hour. Her father sat at the table in his favorite wooden chair—the only chair in the cottage sturdy enough to bear his weight.

"Hello, little cabbage," her father said. He had a canning jar in hand with the remnants of a batch of shine. Prohibition was in full swing, and Rutherford Rose had a new vocation that might have been profitable, had he not been his only customer.

Her mother asked, "Well?"

"Ma'am?"

"Did he pay you?"

Harry had, in fact, given her an advance on her wages, though Elizabeth had no intention of parting with the money. She'd earned it. It was hers. Without answering, she crossed the room to the pantry cupboard. Empty, save some flour.

"Didn't the man feed you?" Constance asked.

"No," Elizabeth admitted.

"Bunk," her mother said. "He thinks you skate around. I warned you." She looked away. "There's already talk, you know."

"I don't skate around, Mother, and I've never done anything to cause you to think so."

"Come give us a kiss, kitten," Rutherford said, his voice slurring. He sat tilted to the side as if ready to fall from his chair.

Constance snorted, shaking her head. "They're not talking about *that*," she said. "Thank the Lord you're working out of residence, rather than boarding with the man." She paused, her scowl deepening. "You know very well that servant jobs are filled by the negroes. It's a mark against your family that you take that kind of work. What was the point of going to college if you end up doing daywork for a cake eater?"

"He's a gentleman!" Elizabeth drew in a breath, struggling to maintain an even voice. "You voiced no objection when I told you of my intention to apply. I will be doing honest work, and the money will help you and Father."

"Not if you raid the cupboard the moment you come home. Between you and your father, I may as well reside with locusts."

Who are these people? Elizabeth thought. Had they always been this way? No, she had good memories. Her father had taken her fishing, once. She hadn't wanted to touch the worms, so he'd threaded the bait for her and hadn't made fun of her squeamishness. They'd sat against the base of a tree near the edge of the stream, bobs floating bright in the morning sunshine. They hadn't talked. Listening to the river was enough. When they came home without a catch, her mother was furious.

Sometimes, her mother's anger sided with her, rather than against her. When she was ten, a boy at school had teased her mercilessly, and when the teasing turned to hair-pulling and other roughhousing, he accidentally tore her blouse. Her mother marched Elizabeth to the boy's home, where she vented at his mother. Walking back, stooped and drained, Constance said, "When someone bullies you, you must ignore them. You are better than any bully. You are my daughter."

Those were the memories Elizabeth held on to. One for each of them, like two bright pennies.

•   •   •

She finished cleaning Harry's cottage, washing his clothing, and hanging it to dry by noon. All that remained was fixing supper. A domestic could clean a house twice the size of the professor's cottage in a day or two. Any competent day worker, arriving at ten and leaving in late afternoon, would have nothing to do on the third day. Besides, the professor was more than Spartan—he was fastidious. Having grown up with Rutherford, who left the proverbial trail of crumbs behind him wherever he went, Elizabeth was amazed to know a man could actually pick up after himself.

The professor would certainly have to cut back her hours, and every day away from the job was another day sequestered with her parents. The thought was abhorrent.

Too soon to start cooking, she gazed at the upright piano. Would it hurt to play a short piece? The professor was busy in his workshop. Would he even hear her? She longed for the piano, so plain yet so obviously well-crafted. She was certain it had a fine sound.

Or would it? The professor didn't play. The piano might be woefully out of tune.

She sat on the small bench and ran her fingers over the keys, barely touching them. Then, tentatively, she hit a middle C. The rich tone melted her heart. She tried a C chord. The sound was pitch perfect. She closed her eyes and began to play.

When she opened her eyes again, the professor stood watching her from the door of his workshop. "You play well," he said.

"I'm sorry—"

"Nonsense. How long have you been playing?"

"I learned in school," she said.

Muskingum College had a piano in the basement of Paul Hall. Her first year in class, she'd been poking at the keys like a child, more out of curiosity than anything else. For a moment, she forgot herself. When she realized that the handsome young man across the room was listening to her, she stopped.

"Don't stop," he told her.

"I don't have any idea what I'm doing," she answered.

"Then I will teach you." That was how she met Walter Raymond, her first beau. He was a tall, handsome boy with a fine heart and a quick smile. He taught her to play, though she soon eclipsed his own skills. "You are a prodigy," he told her.

"You are angling for a kiss," she replied. In time, she gave him many kisses, right up until he shipped off to Europe.

He died in the Battle of Saint-Mihiel.

Thereafter, she continued to play, tutored by the Muskingum music instructor. "You have an instinctive touch," he told her. "Had you been a boy, starting out at an early age, you might have made a name for yourself." She decided he'd meant this as a compliment.

Now, sitting in the professor's cottage, she said, "I haven't had a chance to practice. I am all rust."

"You sounded fine," he assured her. He folded his arms and leaned back against the wall. "What was the melody you were playing?"

"Chopin's *Ballade Number 1 in G Minor, Opus 23*. It's my favorite interlude."

"You've chosen an interlude to play between chores. Charming and ironic." His expression was blank but terribly intense.

Rather than look into those dark eyes, she closed her own and began to play again. The complex melody was comprised of two distinct themes presented through a series of structural changes, from majestic to light and playful, but always rooted in some unnamed sadness. She played from start to finish and then put her hands in her lap. She turned to look at him and was startled by his expression. She had never seen a face so melancholy. Pain etched itself in his eyes, the corners of his mouth, and even the pallor of his skin. When he spoke, his voice cracked. "You may play as often as you like." He turned and walked back into his workshop, closing the door behind him.

•　　•　　•　　•　　•

Each night, the professor walked her home despite her protests, claiming that the fresh air and exercise improved his productivity. She came to enjoy the walks. Unlike the day, when he might go the entire time without speaking two sentences to her, he was almost chatty as they made their way to her parent's cottage. They talked about the stars and planets, flora and fauna, and even the geology of New Concord. "To the south, on the Rice Farm, you can find a large number of fossils in the limestone. Dark shale and coal." He stopped, suddenly perplexed. "Surely this is boring you."

"Not at all," she assured him.

"You are kind to allow me to ramble. I have enjoyed living alone."

"Am I a bother?"

He laughed. An uncommon sound, coming from him. "Not at all. Quite the contrary. I enjoy talking to you!" And then, as if a line had been crossed, he fell silent. Had she overstepped somehow? She was, after all, a servant. The professor did not seem to stand on formalities, but she could not know for sure. It was dark outside, and his face was covered in shadows.

When she arrived at the cottage, she thanked him for his company and went inside. She'd been paid, and now she would have to part with some of the money to her mother. When Elizabeth had announced her new position, Constance made it clear that she expected every penny of her wage to be handed over. Elizabeth refused. "I am going to save a few dollars each week for my future," she explained.

Her mother stared at her in disbelief. "Your future? You spent years at that college. What did the wasted time buy you?" Shaking her head, she added, "No, you will give me every penny. It's time you help out around here."

She could try to convince her mother, but that seemed pointless. She could pretend she'd been paid a lower wage and keep the difference, but that would be a lie. In the end, what she chose to *say* added up to nothing. What she chose to *do* was hold back three dollars a week for herself. She already had coins and a few bills in a thick sock buried behind her dresser drawer. When she had enough money to rent a place of her own, she would leave. She would never come back.

Her mother sat knitting, having purchased a skein of yarn to make a small scarf for Rutherford, though in the winter, he seldom went outside. "Well? Were you paid?"

"Where's Father?"

"He's already out on the roof," she said.

Drunk again.

"I asked you a question. Were you paid?"

"I was," Elizabeth said. She went to place the money on the table, but her mother called for it, hand extended.

"This is what he paid you?" she asked.

"Yes."

Constance Rose frowned at the money as if it had come from her husband's soiled hand. "You are being taken for a fool."

"I do honest work."

"For pennies." The light from the fire made pits and ravines of the lines on her face. "Is this all of it?"

Elizabeth steeled herself. "No, Mother. I kept a few dollars for my savings. I have already discussed this with you."

Constance's mouth dropped open, as if this were the first she'd heard of such a thing. "What are you talking about?"

"I'm talking about my future."

The glow of the fireplace reflected in her mother's eyes—two embers buried in sunken cheeks. When Constance spoke, her voice was parchment. "At this rate, you'll never repay us."

"What debts do you hold against me?"

Her mother snorted her derision. "You live in this house, do you not?"

"I do."

"Then you must earn your keep."

Elizabeth tried to control her breathing. "If the money isn't enough, I can ask for a raise. But I am certainly not a drain on your finances, Mother. I sleep here and little else. I eat like a bird. I clean your—"

Constance lurched in her chair as if to rise. Elizabeth kept her eyes on her mother's needles.

"You *owe* us," she cried. The vitriol in her voice was as real as it was surprising. "For raising you. For clothing and feeding you. For the pain of disappointment that you've been since *your first breath.*" This last, she hissed, sending flecks of spit into the air.

Elizabeth flinched. "I'm your daughter!"

"My *curse.*" Constance set aside her sewing and folded her hands in her lap. She looked directly into Elizabeth's eyes. "But I know you," she said. "You think you can fool me, but you can't. What is he really paying you?"

Elizabeth fought to keep her voice even. "I've told you what I kept for myself."

Constance closed her fist around the money and turned her head away. Elizabeth waited long, silent moments, and then left the room. The three dollars she'd held back burned a hole in her pocket, but she didn't dare move the money to the sock behind her drawer. Her mother would be listening, perhaps lurking just beyond the door. She put the bills under her pillow and got undressed. She would stay awake. In the middle of the night, when everyone else was asleep, she would hide the money with the rest of her savings and then try to rest before heading back to her job.

She lay on her back, under the blanket, and stared at the ceiling without blinking. Her mother's face had frightened her. For as long as she could remember, Constance had been a cold woman. Her outburst this evening had been different. Perhaps her parents had suffered a financial setback of which she was unaware. A setback that put her mother on edge.

Or perhaps tensions between her parents had eaten up her mother's reserve. Rutherford was drinking more these days.

But what could Elizabeth do about any of it? Every last one of her friends from college were married, living in their own homes, enjoying their own lives. She could not stay in this house a moment longer than was necessary. What were her options? Marry? God forbid she end up with a man like her father!

This last thought pulled at her heart. *How ungrateful I am!* She clenched her fists and tried to sleep, but things she might have said and things she might have done kept her awake long into the night, even after her three dollars had been secreted away.

In the early morning, she allowed herself to think of her handsome professor, and in picturing his face, she finally drifted off to sleep.

CHAPTER NINE

A Storm in New Concord/A Storm at Home

Ohio, 1920

Winter came late to New Concord. Instead of snow, icy rain stripped the trees and washed out the roads. Because the sun set early, the professor took a break after supper to escort Elizabeth home. She'd come to enjoy the walks despite the cold air. Bright conversation with the professor was enough to keep her warm.

But every walk ended at her parents' house, a dreadful terminus that left her counting the hours before morning. Constance had, for the most part, stopped speaking to her. Rutherford was pleasant enough—he was a congenial drunk—but when Constance gave him her sharp glance, he too would go silent. Elizabeth felt like a ghost in her own home.

She came close to handing over her savings on more than one occasion. She wondered if she were selfish. A good daughter would care for her parents when they reached their autumn years. She did not, could not love them. Not anymore. That was a mark against her soul, wasn't it? Didn't every mother and father deserve love and care? *As does every child*, she thought.

She'd been honest about the amount of her wage. A lie would have caught in her throat like castor oil. But each week, her mother asked, "This is it? This is what you give me?"

She longed to ask, what of daughters who married? They left homes behind to start a family of their own. If that wasn't a sin, then why was wanting something for herself such a transgression?

Her mother had taken to punctuating her usual silence with cryptic pronouncements. One evening, she looked up from her needles and smiled. "He will never marry you. You know that don't you?" How could her mother have surmised something Elizabeth would not admit to herself? How dare she needle her as if Elizabeth was one of her sewing projects?

Each morning, the sun rose, and Elizabeth escaped the home that seemed more a jail to her now. Arriving at the professor's cottage, she would make sure he had something to eat. He would thank her and take whatever she offered into the workshop. Then, she'd begin her duties.

Monday was laundry day. Tuesday, she mended. On Wednesday, she cleaned the pantry and cupboards. Each day, she washed dishes, watered the plant she'd bought in town, dusted the furniture and mantel, tidied the two bedrooms, swept the floors, attacked cobwebs, set the table, and prepared supper. If the weather permitted, she opened the windows to air out the cottage. She added any small chore she could to make herself useful, even indispensable, lest the professor decide he could do without her.

Twice a week she went into town to buy supplies and pick up the mail. The professor received letters from all over the country and even some from Europe. He never opened them in her presence. They were secreted away in his workshop as soon as they were delivered.

His favorite meal, despite comments to the contrary, was stew and bread. After that first day, he'd insisted she dine with him. He ate with gusto, and in time, managed to put a few necessary pounds on his slender frame. "You are making me fat," he told her, though he was no such thing. Her father was fat. The professor might add another ten pounds and be just right.

One afternoon, the sky darkened with green-gray clouds before the sun began to set, and despite Elizabeth having spent some of the afternoon at the piano, the professor insisted she leave any remaining work for the morning. "More rain, I think," he said, bringing his umbrella.

Outside, the air had the pungent smell of an approaching storm—the fresh and terrible odor of electricity. The professor walked fast without speaking, favoring his stiffened leg with an altered gait. Elizabeth struggled to keep up, disappointed by the storm's intrusion on the best part of her day. The flickering glow of lightning in the distant clouds warned of a coming downpour.

Thunder rolled across the open fields. "Miles away," he assured her. "The sound bounces between the ground and the clouds, which is why it sounds that way." His face had grown paler than usual. Sweat traced his upper lip, though it was freezing outside.

"I hate thunder," Elizabeth said. "You'll think me silly, but it scares me."

"If you can hear the thunder, then you're safe," he said. "When you are lightning's target, you hear nothing. Like an artillery shell."

"Like a shell?"

He ignored her, pushing ahead. The first raindrops came, and he opened the umbrella, motioning her closer. She leaned against him as they walked, their progress slowed now by the storm. She wanted to enjoy the moment and the feeling of his arm bumping into hers, but it was nearly dark. The wind made the rain dance. The professor struggled to find a position that would afford them both protection.

More thunder. She shivered. "It's getting closer, isn't it?"

"I suppose so." He squinted at the road ahead. "Ten more minutes, and you'll be in your house, safe and sound."

"I hate to think of you walking home alone in this."

He laughed nervously. "I don't mind it. The sound of thunder reminds me of France. Almost like home."

"You mean during the war?" He'd never mentioned the war before.

Again, he ignored the question. "If this weather continues, you may want to consider staying in tomorrow. If you don't come by, I'll understand."

She started to protest, but a flash of lightning ripped the sky. The thunderclap, almost instantaneous, deafened her. Before she could react, the professor threw her to the ground face-first in the mud. Her nose bounced on the ground, blinding her for a moment. She turned her head sideways to breathe but couldn't. Something pressed on top of her. She tried to push herself up but didn't have the strength.

On the verge of panic, she squirmed in the mud, realizing that the weight pushing down on her was the professor. After a few moments, he lifted himself up, first on all fours and then to a sitting position. She took in a deep breath. Rain had begun to fall in earnest. Wind rushed across the open field, sending the rain sideways.

"I am so sorry," he said, trying to stand. "I cannot apologize enough." He offered her a trembling hand, pulling her to her feet. "I've ruined your clothing."

"Not at all," she said, though mud coated her coat and dress.

"Your nose is bleeding," He reached for his pocket where a handkerchief might be found, but he'd not brought one. He patted the pocket and then looked away.

"I'm all right, Professor." She brushed at her coat, smearing mud. "Really."

"I must explain myself," he said. Then he was silent.

The wind swirled around them, driving rain up under the umbrella. He hurried along the wet road. She slipped once, but he caught her by the elbow. "Thank you," she said. He seemed not to hear.

The last five minutes of the journey were wet, cold, and uncomfortable. She almost welcomed the sight of her parents' front door. She wanted to say something—anything—but the professor reversed direction, limping off into the dark without a word. Elizabeth stood with a hand to her mouth, a feeling of dread nearly overwhelming her.

Into the cottage and out of the rain, the dread intensified. Her father sat in his wooden chair, an empty glass in his hand. His sullen gaze frightened her. "I was worried," he said, his tongue slow and thick in his mouth.

"No need to worry," she said, removing her coat.

He pointed at her clothing. "Seems like you were rolling around in the mud with your professor friend."

"We fell. The storm."

"Fell together, did you?" He licked his lips, glanced at the glass, and shook his head.

Constance came shuffling from her bedroom, her hands knotted together. She smiled like a cat with a mouse under its paw. "You're back early." She looked Elizabeth up and down. "You are a sight."

"Yes, I suppose so," Elizabeth said. She touched her sore nose and winced. "I fell."

"I heard." Her mother's smile widened. "Quite a sight indeed."

"The storm." Elizabeth's voice was a croak.

"Well, there's a storm here at home," her mother said. "Let me ask you something. What do you take me for?"

No answer.

"I told you, child. Every penny. I wanted to see *every single penny* of your wage."

Her money. Elizabeth brushed past her mother. Her room was in shambles. Bedcovers were torn away, the mattress pulled aside, and the drawers to her small bureau had been pulled out and stacked on the floor.

The sock holding her savings was gone.

"Years of college, and that was the best hiding place you could imagine?" Her mother's voice was more cheerful than it had been in weeks. "I told you. You are not smart enough by half."

Elizabeth turned, a cold fury seizing her. "That money was mine. Return it now."

Her mother shuffled forward, placing her face less than a foot away. "How dare you talk to me in that tone of voice! Who do you think you are? You are in *my* house. You will do what *I* say."

"This is—"

"Close your mouth." Her mother's spit flecked her cheek. "Things are going to change here. You went to college and came out with the mind of a pea. You should have been working and helping out. Instead, you wasted your time. What job do you have after all your fine plans? Cleaning a man's toilet?"

Elizabeth looked around the room. A room that was no longer hers. Everything she'd owned had been rifled through. Nothing here belonged to her. She stooped over and grabbed a few pieces of clothing. She would take what she absolutely needed and nothing else. The rest could be replaced.

"Are you listening to me?" her mother demanded.

"Yes, Mother." She stuffed the clothing into her otherwise empty shoulder bag.

"Exactly what do you think you're doing?"

"I'm leaving."

Her mother's mocking laugh made her skin crawl. "You're not going anywhere." She grabbed Elizabeth by the shoulder, but Elizabeth twisted away. Constance grabbed for her hair next. "You're staying here!"

Elizabeth pulled free with a cry.

"Rutherford!" Constance called. "Rutherford!"

"Don't be a Dumb Dora," her father said, slurring.

Elizabeth crossed the room to the door.

"You've nowhere to go!" Constance cried. "No one will have you!"

She opened the door to a blast of rain. She hesitated only for a moment—long enough to gaze in her father's direction—and then plunged into the darkness.

Elizabeth walked to the road, her shoes making a sucking sound in the mud. In her hurry to leave her mother's house, she'd left her coat behind. She crossed her arms over her chest and made her way as best she could, shivering uncontrollably.

The storm outside played a countermelody to the storm in her heart. The first movement, driven by anger, gave way to a second movement—one of despair. Her mother had been right. She had nowhere to go.

A sudden gust made her slip, and she dropped her shoulder bag. Tempted to leave the muddied bag behind, she stood swaying in the wind, tears streaming down her face. "I have nothing of my own," she whispered.

"Everything I have belongs to someone else." She closed her eyes for a moment. Rain had soaked her through.

She could go back to her parents' house, or she could move forward. To stand still in the rain would be absurd. She picked up the bundle and continued along the road.

She would knock on Mrs. Hartley's door. The good widow would not turn her away. Having a destination allowed Elizabeth to move with urgency, one foot in front of the other. She would sleep at the widow's home. In the morning, an answer to her dilemma would come to her.

Given her dire situation, she couldn't work for the professor in the morning. He would worry when she didn't arrive. She looked off in the distance. She ought to let him know. The trajectory of her thoughts carried her past the turnoff to Mrs. Hartley's. She would explain what had happened and assure him that she'd be back on the job within a day.

Just as well, she thought. She hadn't liked seeing him stride off into the night, silent. She tried to think about what had happened when the lightning struck, but it was too cold to consider anything but her misery. The rain seeped into her skin and bones, leaving her trembling. By the time the professor's cottage came into view, she'd begun to pray he would let her stay. The thought of doubling back to Mrs. Hartley's made her want to collapse.

She did not recall knocking on the door, but she was suddenly inside, wrapped in a blanket, and placed on a chair in front of the dying fire. The professor put a dry log on, poking the embers to bring up the flame. Then he rushed off to the kitchen. She shook, eyes closed, and thought she might pass out. A cup of hot tea appeared in her hands. She sipped it gratefully. "I need to tell you—"

"Tomorrow," he said. "First, we'll get you warm. Then, you'll sleep. In the bed. I'll stay in the workshop."

"I can't take your bed—"

"You have the wrong impression," he said. "I work most every night. I do not sleep." He put a hand gently to her cheek, a kindness that nearly made her weep. "I have things to tell you as well," he continued. "But we need not rush into our explanations, do we? A time to every purpose, and that time is tomorrow."

CHAPTER TEN

Inside the Workshop/A New Arrangement

Ohio, 1920

During the night, Elizabeth developed a fever. Harry went out in the early morning and returned with a physician. Doctor Kemp seemed put out to have been rousted from his home at such an hour, but after a brief examination of his patient, he became all business. He put a thermometer in her mouth and waited the long minutes necessary to bring the device up to temperature. He took her pulse. He asked her questions, which she answered slowly, owing to a general loss of energy.

Harry followed the doctor into the main room, closing the bedroom door behind him and feeling sick with worry.

"She is dehydrated from the fever," Doctor Kemp told Harry. "She must try to sip water. Don't let her take in too much at once. The heaves would only exacerbate her situation."

"I left her with water at the nightstand. What about tea?"

Doctor Kemp tugged at his goatee—a scrubby tuft of salt-and-pepper that curled to the left. "Tea is fine." He paused. "She doesn't have the Spanish influenza. The symptoms don't align. She has the fatigue and chills, but there's no cough."

"Her symptoms came on suddenly. Isn't that an indication—"

"You yourself said she was out in the storm. Count her lucky *not* to have the influenza. Keep her hydrated and make her rest." He put a hand on Harry's shoulder. "I've seen my share of influenza victims. Their symptoms are more severe. Her fever is worrisome, but I believe she'll be fine."

"Thank you, Doctor," Harry said. "I'm grateful for your visit."

Doctor Kemp donned his coat and scratched at the nightshirt underneath. He'd hurried out of his home without dressing fully. His tweed cap lay on the table. "I'm going now," he announced, grabbing the cap. "Mrs. Kemp will have breakfast waiting for me, and I'll eat it, warm or cold."

"I could cook for you," Harry said.

"No, no, Mrs. Kemp would regard that as a culinary infidelity." He chuckled.

"Can she eat?" Harry asked, nodding toward the bedroom door.

"Of course. As soon as she cares to." The doctor gave him a squinty glance. "The gentleman cooking for the maid?"

"Friend, too, I think."

The doctor gave him a tired smile and left him to his duties.

Harry hadn't opened the cupboard door since Elizabeth had come to work for him. Now he gazed in surprise at the stock of ingredients. He'd never had so much to work with! He decided on biscuits, which ought to be simple enough. Flour, fat, salt, baking powder and water. If he'd had butter, he'd have cut some into the mix, but bacon fat made a savory biscuit.

The first batch burned.

"This oven is not my friend," he whispered, starting over. By the time the second batch was ready, he could hear Elizabeth stirring behind the door.

She came out wrapped head to toe in a blanket. "Something smells wonderful," she said.

"Hungry, then? That's a good sign." He sat her at the table and brought her a cup of tea, a glass of water, a small plate of biscuits, and a jar of jam. Elizabeth sat still, staring at the food. "Is something wrong?" Harry asked.

She picked up a biscuit and took a bite. "I don't like biscuits," she said. "But I like these. Are you certain they're biscuits?"

He burst out laughing—something he hadn't done for some time. She sat smiling, despite her apparent wooziness.

"Very funny," he said. "I think you're going to be fine." He pulled up a chair and grabbed one of the biscuits.

Elizabeth ate slowly, sipping at her water and tea, watching him. "You seem wholly consumed in consuming your biscuits," she said.

He looked up, startled.

"I'm sorry," she said.

"Not at all. A biscuit, once completed, must be completely eaten."

He watched her curious smile and wondered what it meant.

They continued breakfast in silence. Her sideways glances and deep breaths were surely leading to something. He feared that he knew what she was going to say. He must explain himself. "Coming here last night—"

"I'm so sorry about that, sir. I only meant to explain why I wouldn't be here in the morning."

"Yet here you are," he said, smiling. "How is your nose?"

She touched her nose tentatively. "It will be fine, I think. Does it look dreadful?"

He shook his head. "Of course not. But I treated you roughly last night, and you must allow me to explain. The lightning—"

"Struck quite close to us, didn't it?"

"Yes." Harry sat back. How to tell her this? He'd told no one. "I had a bad time of it in the war," he started. Then he was silent. Elizabeth sat waiting, a kindness in her large brown eyes that quickened his heart. In his entire life, he'd never known anyone so beautiful. She had an oval face and gently curved jaw with the pale skin of an angel. Her lips had a natural pink and cinnamon hue. When she laughed, a dimple bracketed the right side of her smile.

The thought of telling her everything paralyzed him.

"Have you spoken of the war to anyone?" she finally asked.

"No." He looked away. To tell her, he must meet her gaze. "I did not do much fighting in the war. I dug trenches. I repaired breastworks. Long, unending days and nights. I did not fight the Germans. I fought mud and rats. Then, one day, a shell struck, killing my best friend."

"Is that how your leg was damaged?"

"Yes. Set it on fire." She raised an eyebrow. "A tiny fire. After that, I went to the hospital. That's where I stayed until the end of the war."

"Not such a small burn, then."

Harry shook his head. "I was in the hospital even after the leg was treated." He closed his eyes before plunging on. "They call it shell shock."

"I've heard of that."

"You can understand why, then, when someone in town calls me a war hero, it leaves me feeling like a fraud."

"I see," she said. "Did you not serve? Were you not wounded?"

He didn't answer.

"I'm told you received a Wound Ribbon."

He gave her a small nod.

"Then, you are a decorated war hero."

"Not a hero," he mumbled.

"Tell me," she said, taking his hand. "How many men do you have to kill to qualify as a hero?" Harry was silent. "So, you were wounded, both inside and out. How are you healing now?"

"For the most part, I am recovered," he continued. "But on occasion, I suffer a relapse. I have difficulty tracking time. Talking to most people leaves me drained." He pulled his hand away, regretfully. "When the lightning struck last night, my body acted before my mind could process what was happening. For a moment, I was back in the trenches. You were caught in my mental cross fire." He reached for another biscuit but pushed the plate away instead. Outside, the sun was unseasonably bright. "I wonder. Did you come here last night to give me notice?"

She looked startled. "What do you mean?"

"I behaved abominably."

"You certainly did not."

"I threw you to the ground."

She leaned forward until he turned and looked her way. "And you covered me with your body. To protect me. It was a gallant thing to do."

Harry winced. He took a deep breath and decided to change the subject. "Why did you come here so late, soaked to the bone without a coat or jacket?"

She sat back and shivered, as if the mere memory of her walk in the dark was enough to chill her. She explained that she and her parents were estranged.

"You've been a generous employer. I set money aside for my future. My mother laid claim to the money. Perhaps I was being selfish—"

"Nonsense," he said. It was Harry's turn to defend her. "In these modern times, a woman may well refuse to be dependent on her parents for support. That is how you strike me."

"I'm not a flapper," she said, her voice low.

Harry laughed. Her expression lightened at the sound of it. "Good God, no. Far from it. You work for a living, like any responsible man would." He sighed. "Were things so bad, you couldn't go back for your coat?"

Elizabeth nodded, shivering again.

"Well, then. We must do something to address your situation." He pointed to the room to the left, empty, save for a few boxes. "That room will be yours. We'll go into town and find a bed and dresser for you. We'll also shop for clothes. Something new and fashionable."

She blushed. "You must think me a case."

"Not at all. I'm going to tell you something, and I don't want you to become angry. Can you promise me?"

She squinted at him without answering.

"Well, then, I'll have to take my chances. This morning, while bringing the doctor, I inquired about your family—" Her stricken expression stopped him for a moment. "I did not pry. I simply wanted an idea of what problem might have driven you out into the storm." It was his turn to take her hand. "You needn't talk about it. But I suspect you've good reason to want to be away." He sat back. "And here we are. Away." He searched her face for a reaction but found none. "Do you have reservations?"

"This is your home," she said. "I would be moving from someone else's home to a different someone else's home."

"Ahh." Harry paused to consider this. Was this the moment he'd waited for? The moment when he could tell her? She'd certainly given him an opening. Yes. He wouldn't wait another minute. "I would like to think that you could eventually feel like this place was yours as well. And I think I know how to do that."

"So, you'll show me the workshop?" she asked.

"What?" He sat back, flummoxed.

"Your workshop. If I were to share this house with you, there can't be areas that are off limits." She sniffed. "Besides, there are problems with the arrangement. How will we share a single bathroom?"

"One problem at a time," he said, standing. He walked to the workshop door and opened it.

She padded across the floor, still wrapped in the blanket, and peered inside. Electric bulbs illuminated the room. A workbench ran the full length of the room's left side. On the back wall, floor-to-ceiling bookshelves held not only printed material, but a dizzying array of wires and electrical parts, along with several devices she did not recognize. Tools hung from a pegboard on the far-right wall. A second workbench sat between the pegboard and the door. Two copper antennae, shaped in spiral forms, rested on the bench. Next to them, she saw an instrument she thought she recognized. "Is that a Ritchie's photometer?"

Harry felt his jaw drop. He stared at Elizabeth, stunned. "How on earth do you know what that is?" he asked.

"You brought one to class," she said. "At Muskingum."

He put a hand to the smaller workbench, as if to prop himself up. "You're a Muskie?"

"Class of 1918," she said.

He took a deep breath, then let it out at once before taking a second deep breath. "You have surprised me more than once with your cleverness, but I never guessed you had a degree. How thick-headed of me! You must think me a dolt." He paused. "You graduated, did you not?" She nodded. "How did you afford the tuition?"

"I was sponsored by your Professor Brympton."

This confounded Harry. "I don't understand. I'm certain that I've mentioned him to you on more than one occasion. How did I not know this?"

She looked away, uncertain. "I was applying for a housekeeper's position. I didn't feel it appropriate to use Muskingum as a shared connection. Later, I was ashamed to tell you. I'm . . . I'm a housekeeper."

"Dear Mr. Brympton," Harry mused. He wished the man were here, so they could share this happy coincidence. "So, why aren't you working in the science field?"

Elizabeth slumped in place, nearly dropping her blanket. She tightened her grip. "I tried. This may come as a surprise to you, but jobs in the sciences are hard to find, and women are not at the top of the hiring list."

"Did you try Zanesville?"

"I tried *everywhere*." Her voice carried a bitter edge. She stopped and stood straighter. "I'm sorry, Professor. For a moment, I sounded like my mother."

He shook his head. "You sounded like someone who visited too many dead ends." He glanced at the photometer. "You say that I showed you one of these?"

"Yes. In class."

"You took a class from me?"

"I did," she said. "You were my favorite professor."

"I feel certain I would remember you."

Elizabeth looked disappointed.

"Wait! A braid? You had a single braid, draped behind you." She nodded, smiling. "Oh, I remember you now! You've changed, of course. You were so very . . . *young*. Time has, well, you've changed. I remember you, though. I remember." He smiled slyly. "You challenged everything I said in class."

"I'm sorry! I was excited by the things you taught—"

Harry laughed again, and it was as if he were young again and the trenches had never happened. "What do you imagine science is? Questions and answers. And the answers must always be revisited because many of them are wrong! No dull-eyed student, you! You wanted to know the *why* of *everything*." He began to pace, words spilling out of him. "Well then, you were sent to me by Divine Providence. I could make good use of an assistant. Someone to take notes, keep my journals, untangle my thoughts, and witness my results. I require a second set of eyes. I require verification of my results. You can do that, can't you? I'm certain you can. Of course, I'll need your usual help with the household things." He stopped. "This will involve a great deal of work. We will have to adjust your salary. And you *must* reside here. I do not want to lose work to snow days."

Then he noticed the tears welling in her eyes.

"What's wrong? Does my idea not suit you?"

"Yes. Yes, it suits me very well." She dabbed at her eyes with her fingertips. "Last night, I had no prospects. I don't know what to say."

Harry shrugged. "Say yes."

She curtsied, and then staggered a little. He caught her elbow. Carefully, he steered her to the bedroom. "I was charged with seeing that you rest. Look what a terrible job I've done! You must go to bed immediately. If you are to take on your new duties, you'll need to recover. Don't worry. I will take care of everything." He drew back the bedspread and waited until she climbed on the bed, blanket and all.

"I . . . I am so grateful. I can't tell you how much this means to me. I show up at your door half-drowned—"

"Applesauce," he said. "Please rest. We have work to do."

When he reached the door, he heard her voice crack. "But I need to say this." He stopped. "This chance. This is all I could have ever wanted. This was my dream."

He beamed at her and then left the room, closing the door behind him.

On the other side of the door, he stopped, rubbing his eyes. He hadn't expected any of this, and now his words caught up with him. He'd meant to say something entirely different. But the look in her eyes told him that this was what she wanted, and he wouldn't take it away from her. Not for anything.

If, instead, he'd told her he loved her and that he wanted to make her his wife, then everything else he'd offered her would be suspect. He would not introduce that doubt. His hopes could wait. He would not take her triumph away.

CHAPTER ELEVEN

Madame Phoenix/A Late Night Carriage Ride

Ohio, 1920

"Where are we going?" she asked. The professor stood near the front door wearing his threadbare overcoat. He did not wear a hat, which, like his lack of facial hair, was unusual. He did not seem to have any concern for style. *Function,* he had told her, *is more important than fashion.* She planned to nudge him in the direction of current trends, but that would be a long-term project. Elizabeth was a patient woman.

Some matters, however, eluded her capacity for patience. Before assisting in the workshop, the professor wanted her to have the "necessary context" to properly understand his work. What that meant was a mystery. "Dress in black," he told her.

The few pieces of clothing she'd taken from home were colored in plain earth tones. He'd insisted on black, so they went shopping. He chose a clothier in Zanesville. Her black, bias-cut silk evening dress draped in graceful folds over her figure. Trying it on, she scarcely recognized herself in the mirror. The woman who stared back at her was elegant and sophisticated. "This dress says two things," the professor told her. "You are rich, and you are in mourning." He did not explain, launching into one of his extended silences instead.

Back at the cottage, he handed her a slip of paper, saying, "Please read this. Memorize what's here. If you are asked anything that extends beyond the information contained here, you will use your imagination and make it up. Try to be convincing."

Name: Doris Blake Hutchins
Age: 23
Husband: Derek Hutchins, died in the Argonne Forest 1918. Non-smoker.
Father: Horace Blake, owner of Blake Manufacturing. Overweight. Enjoyed his cigars and his whiskey.
Mother: Belinda Blake, deceased. Died of heart disease.
Background: You are widowed. You miss your husband more than words can say. Your father, also recently deceased, left you with a massive endowment, which you would gladly trade just to speak with your beloved husband again.

"I don't understand," she told him.

"You will. Now, memorize that page."

During her recovery from fever, the professor had been busy. He'd purchased a bed and small bureau in town, along with a wall mirror and a short list of necessaries that she'd left behind in her escape from her parents. Now, in her room, she memorized the professor's list while dressing. Horace Blake sounded uncomfortably like her own father.

When she was ready, the professor stood by the door. Since he hadn't answered her question, she repeated herself. "Where are we going?"

"Tonight, we pay a visit to Madame Phoenix. Remember your role."

Then, they were off. A horse and carriage took them to the far side of New Concord. The driver, hired for the night, stepped to the carriage door to help Elizabeth down, extending a gloved hand. She nearly stumbled, but the professor was at her side to steady her.

"What is this place?" she asked. They'd stopped in front of an old Victorian home. In the dark, it was impossible to tell the color of the house. The faded paint might have been green or gray or even blue. The façade above the porch steps was broken. Shingles were missing. The rain gutters were hanging in spots. But the walkway to the front steps was weeded and swept clean. A woman waited at the front door, hands clasped around a candle. Her gray hair, wrapped tight atop her head, matched her severe expression.

"Madame Phoenix," the professor whispered. "The spiritualist."

Inside, Elizabeth was escorted into a drawing room. The walls were draped in heavy velvet curtains. A candle in the center of an oval table was the only illumination beyond the one carried by Madame Phoenix. The room was irregularly shaped, such that the corners were indistinct. Elizabeth's eyes were drawn to the candle on the table and the circle of faces around it. Four others were already seated, including a businessman, an elderly woman, and a pair of young women who looked enough alike to be sisters.

Elizabeth and the professor sat next to each other at the table. The woman who'd greeted them at the door blew out her candle and sat at the head of the table. "We are all here now," she said. "I am"—she paused for a moment as if to prolong the introduction—"Madame Phoenix. I will be your spirit guide this evening. We are brave souls who seek knowledge from those who have passed beyond the veil. It is not required that all believe. Indeed, we are joined by Professor Browning, an old friend who remains a skeptic, despite his inability to explain what you will see here tonight . . . the unexplainable."

The professor nodded in apparent deference.

"It is of utmost importance," she continued, "that once hands are joined, you do not break the circle. What we do here tonight is not without risk. Only by maintaining contact can we ensure the safety of those of you brave enough to explore death's mysteries."

The candle flickered, casting uncertain shadows.

"We shall begin in a moment. There are difficulties in communicating with those we have lost. For that reason, I will ask questions of you that require a simple yes or no answer. If those you hope to communicate with are present, they will speak to me, and I will pass their messages on. Again, I ask you *not* to break contact. In a moment, we'll begin. Professor Browning? Will you assist me?"

The professor crossed the room. Madame Phoenix handed him two pieces of rope and then sat down in a wooden chair, her forearms placed along the arms of the chair. "What do you have for me this evening, Professor?"

"A round turn and two half hitches," the professor said. "This knot was taught to me by a sailor who claimed that it never failed throughout the entire history of nautical pursuits." He began tying Madame Phoenix to the chair with elaborate knots. When he finished, he returned to the table.

"Please join hands, and do not let go until our session is over."

Elizabeth took the professor's hand. It was warm, and the touch made her smile. On her left, the elderly woman offered her tiny, bent hand, dry as paper. Though the house was old, and might ordinarily creak and moan, the room was silent. Perhaps the heavy curtains acted as a damper.

Elizabeth waited. Nothing happened. She glanced to her right. The professor watched Madame Phoenix with a curious intensity.

Finally, Madame Phoenix asked, "Are there spirits here tonight who would communicate with our brave circle?"

No answer.

Madame Phoenix waited. Elizabeth looked around her. The candlelight did not reach the corners of the room. The room smelled faintly of mold. Her nose twitched, and she longed to rub it, but she'd been told not to let go.

"Are there spirits who would communicate with us this evening?" Madame Phoenix asked again. Again, silence. The professor glanced her way.

Then the candle went out.

"Maintain contact with each other," Madame Phoenix warned. "Spirits, we ask you to make yourself known to us, so that we may begin to communicate. Are you willing? Rap once for yes and twice for no."

A single rap sent a chill along Elizabeth's spine.

"We begin then. I am a clairaudient. I hear the voices of those who have died and pass along their messages. We have a new member of our brave party this evening. As a courtesy, we will begin our search with her. Doris Hutchins?"

No answer. The professor nudged her ankle under the table. *I'm Doris Hutchins!* Elizabeth thought. "I'm here," she said. Her voice came out in a croak.

"Who would you like to speak to, Mrs. Hutchins?"

"My husband," she answered. "My dear husband, Derek."

Madame Phoenix called out, "Derek Hutchins? I would speak to Derek Hutchins. Are you here?"

The single rapping sound came from across the room.

"I would vouchsafe his identity before continuing," Madame Phoenix said, her voice as solemn as a hearse. "Did your husband smoke?"

"No, no he didn't," Elizabeth said, wondering at the professor's magic. How had he known she would ask the question?

Madame Phoenix moaned. "I am told that your husband abhorred the habit. He thought it disgusting."

The professor tapped her ankle under the table with his foot. "Why, yes. That's right!" she said.

"I am confused. There is an image of someone else smoking. Did your father smoke?"

"Yes. Cigars. He loved cigars."

"I can see an image of an older man, smoking a cigar and drinking whiskey."

"My father loved whiskey," Elizabeth said. *A truth at last.*

"Your husband wishes me to tell you that he mourns the life you never had together. He misses you. He aches for you every day."

Elizabeth thought of her first beau, Walter Raymond. He'd died in the war, the same as the fictitious Derek Hutchins. Here in the dark, blanketed by silence, she felt a curious surge of emotion. Her voice cracked when she spoke. "Derek, oh Derek!"

"Your husband died overseas. In the war."

"Yes," Elizabeth said. How did the woman know that? Surely, the professor had said as much before bringing her to the séance. Besides, *there was no husband.* This woman was a fraud. Is that what the professor wanted her to see? Surely, that bit of news wasn't worth the cost of a black silk dress! The medium continued, and Elizabeth found herself becoming angry.

"I'm getting something about the number two from your husband. Did he have two siblings, or did he perhaps—"

"No." Elizabeth's answer was sharp. She waited for another tap at the ankle from the professor, but none came. The professor held her hand as gently as before.

"Your husband's wound—"

"Derek wasn't wounded," she said. "He contracted the Spanish flu and died in a French hospital." There was something horrible and twisted about these proceedings, and she would not play along.

"Ahhh. Of course," Madame Phoenix said. "I understand now." As if to prove her claim to the name she'd given herself, she recovered, rising from the ashes. "He did not say *two*. He said *flu*. Of course."

Elizabeth was silent.

"I am losing contact now," Madame Phoenix said. "He wants me to tell you something about a key, but I . . . I can't finish."

"A key?" Elizabeth asked.

"I've lost him. I am sorry," Madame Phoenix said. "Perhaps another night. There are others who wish to speak." She cleared her throat. "Mrs. Osborne? Can you hear me?"

The old woman grasping Elizabeth's left hand answered. "Yes?"

Elizabeth strained to see in the darkness but couldn't make out the medium. "Mrs. Osborne!" Madame Phoenix's voice carried a hint of panic. "Your granddaughter. She—"

"I'm here, Emily," the old woman said. "Oh, my dear, I'm here!"

"Oh! I'm being pulled away. This is most unusual!" Madame Phoenix cried. Her voice actually traveled across the room from left to right. Elizabeth froze. Cold silver shot through her veins.

To the professor's right, a pale blue light appeared. The form took the shape of a little girl dressed in a nightgown. Her image faded, and then returned. A beautiful spectral child, holding a flower in her hand, standing at the end of a long, dark hallway.

Elizabeth squeezed the professor's hand.

Then, the image was gone. The curtains ruffled as if a breeze had somehow entered the house, chilling them all. A moan from Madame Phoenix signaled the end of the séance. The businessman struck a match and lit the candle at the center of the table. By its light, Elizabeth could see Madame Phoenix slumped in her chair, still tied by the wrists.

"Are you all right, Madame?" the businessman asked, rushing to her side.

"Yes, yes Mr. Purdy. I am fine. Tired, but fine."

The professor joined the businessman, untying the medium from her chair.

"I saw my granddaughter!" Mrs. Osborne gushed. "I recognized her immediately!"

Elizabeth sat back and watched. The sisters—for she'd decided that's what they must be—seemed horrified by the vision of the spectral child. They sat next to one another, arms entwined, trembling. "I saw her with my own eyes," one said, her voice filled with wonder.

"Mr. Purdy. I'm so sorry we didn't hear from your sister tonight. Mine is an inexact science. I cannot guarantee contact, as you know."

He took her hand, patting it. "I am so glad I was here, Madame Phoenix. The séance was a revelation! A miracle!" Madame Phoenix gave him a weak smile.

The spot where the spirit appeared was curtained, much like the rest of the room. The professor moved toward the front room, where Madame Phoenix had placed a pitcher of tea and a tray of Zu Zu ginger snaps. The businessman escorted the medium and Mrs. Osborne out of the room, closely followed by the sisters, leaving Elizabeth to glance around. Though she was certain that some form of trickery was involved, the sight of the ghost girl had frightened her, and she was reluctant to remain in the room alone.

Back in the foyer, the conversation continued. "I hope my knots were not too tight, Madame," the professor said, cookie in hand.

Madame Phoenix rubbed her wrists and gave him a rueful smile. "No, of course not, Professor."

Elizabeth came to his side. Madame Phoenix turned to appraise her. "Your dress is exquisite, my dear. You are a lovely vision. I am so sorry I could not continue to channel your departed husband's thoughts. As the professor can attest, as he is a frequent visitor to my parlor, there are nights that I simply cannot make connections."

"An inexact science," the professor agreed.

• • • • •

"I am at a loss to find any meaning in this evening's events," Elizabeth said as the carriage driver took them home. The night sky was clear and cold. Stars lit the way without the aid of even a sliver of moon. Under different circumstances, this ride might have been a most wonderful ending to the evening. "I would have been convinced by the medium's performance had I not known that Derek Hutchins was a complete fiction."

"A good performance, though? She's very accomplished."

"Yes. I assume she had an accomplice?"

The professor shrugged. "Yes, for part of the show."

The carriage rolled ahead, wheels crunching the frozen ground. Elizabeth shivered. "I suppose I know how she did some of the tricks." She turned to him. "But you did tricks of your own. How did you know she would ask about my pretend husband's attitude toward smoking? Did she ask you in advance?"

"No. And no magic was involved. As she said, I am a frequent visitor, and she tends to repeat herself with new clients."

"Clients? Am I a client now?"

"You want to know more about the mysterious key, do you not?"

"There is no key," Elizabeth said.

"Of course not. But if you were more gullible, you might pay to get an answer. A good investment, if the key opened a box full of stock certificates or gold coins."

"So, Madame Phoenix gave me a taste, in hopes I'd want to eat the whole cake?"

The professor nodded. He shifted his sitting position and rubbed his hands together. "It's cold."

"Yes, and I'm very glad you hired a carriage." Elizabeth stared up at the night sky. "The stars are striking in the winter."

"Beautiful," he said, looking straight at her. "So, have you figured out how she did her tricks?"

"Some. The accomplice rapped the answers to her question?"

"No, that was Madame Phoenix herself."

"But you tied her. Are you the accomplice you spoke of?"

"No," he laughed. "The ropes are a diversion. The more creative the knot, the more convincing her imprisonment. I tie her wrists, and then loop the remaining rope around the chair. But the chair? The arms of the chair swing out from behind, at the joint where they fix to the chair back. Once the lights are out, she swings the arms out and slides my careful knots free. She walks around the room, ropes dangling from her wrists. When the performance ends, she slides the loops back onto the chair's arms and then positions the arms in place."

"And that is how her voice traveled. How do you know this?"

"I knew my knots were tight. Thus, they must be misdirection. A glance at the chair itself verified my suspicions." He chuckled. "I make a show of bringing a new knot each time I attend. It's part of the reason she tolerates my return. My skepticism allows her other guests to be gullible."

"I see," she said. "What about the candle?"

"I believe Mr. Purdy assists her in that matter. He doesn't need his hands to blow the flame out. I sometimes tease the matter by watching him directly, which causes poor Madame Phoenix to call for the spirits several times before I turn away and let the poor man do his job."

The carriage horse snorted, and the driver muttered something in response. "All right. How did she manage the ghost child? That was unnerving."

"It's a good trick. She's only done it once before. I had heard of such a trick being performed in the Grand Guignol Theater in the Pigalle District of Paris. There, they turned a poor woman into a skeleton of bones."

"Not really?" she asked.

"The trick involves a sheet of glass angled so that the reflection is visible, but not the object itself. The actual girl, the accomplice I mentioned, stands to the side, lit from above so that her image appears on the glass, superimposed on whatever can be seen *through* the glass—in this case, a hallway."

"But I saw no glass in the room."

"But you saw curtains, easily drawn."

"Drawn by the woman *not* tied to a chair."

"Exactly."

Elizabeth sat back. "So, you go there to debunk a charlatan?"

"Not at all. Madame Phoenix, also known as Eudora Waters, asks little for her entertainments. On occasion, she lands a big fish, and that fish gets a visit from a concerned professor who explains that, though no real harm's done, it would be a good idea not to write any large cheques to the madame. As to Eudora's finances, her professor friend has been generous."

"How do you know this woman?"

"Eudora is the daughter of a fairly wealthy woman named Nesbit. Her mother was kind to me when I was just a boy. Young Eudora married a scoundrel who lost most of their money betting bangtails. With no money left for the racetrack, he disappeared. Opportunities for survival are limited for women, as you discovered during your job search. Her performances are skilled. I consider her an accomplished illusionist and am pleased to patronize her."

Elizabeth shook her head. "I don't always understand you."

"Some things are a mystery," he said.

She nudged him. "Why did she insist on one-word answers?"

"A yes or no enables her to make obvious follow-up statements. If she'd asked why your poor dead husband didn't smoke, you might have said the habit repulsed him.

She'd have answered that, true, the habit repulsed him. No revelation there. But with your yes or no, she's free to make a logical extension of the answer and present it as proof of her clairaudience. The request for one-word answers is a warning sign, in any case."

Elizabeth shifted on the carriage bench to face him. "Does she know that you are on to her?"

"No. Each time I come armed with a new knot. That's a bit of misdirection on my part. She focuses on the ropes, instead of my understanding of her theater."

"One more question. Why were we there?" Elizabeth asked.

"That is, of course the pertinent question. What is my fascination with Madame Phoenix's tricks?"

"No, your fascination is more misdirection. What did you want me to learn?"

The professor tilted his head. Little more than a silhouette, yet she had the distinct impression that he was smiling. "Very good. I attend Madame Phoenix's performances to observe her clients."

"But why?"

"I wish to know if the project I've chosen to pursue is worthwhile. One method of answering that question involves utility. Does the project serve a need?" He shifted in his seat to better face her. "Why do you suppose people visit a medium? The spiritualist craze ended decades ago. Most sensible people are skeptical. Yet, Madame Phoenix has a dedicated following."

"Why indeed?"

"In observing the clientele, I found three distinct motivations. Some of her guests, like the two sisters at the séance this evening, are simply looking for entertainment."

"If you call being frightened a form of entertainment."

The professor went on, ignoring her comment. "Poor Mrs. Osborne demonstrated the second motivation. Her granddaughter Emily died very young, a victim of the Spanish flu. A quarter of the children in our United States die before the age of five. Heartbreak on a catastrophic level."

A pause, and then, "Parents, siblings, husbands and wives all die. I've listened to the surviving family members at Madame Phoenix's table. *I'm sorry. I miss you. Can you forgive me?* The answers they get are repetitive as well. *I'm all right. Yes, I forgive you. I love you.*"

"She performs a service of sorts," Elizabeth said, a touch of reluctance in her voice. "And what is the third motivation?"

"The desire to know if the human spirit survives. We fear death, so we long for proof of immortality. Life after death."

Elizabeth sat quietly, waiting. One of the professor's more bothersome habits was doling out information a piece at a time. She supposed that he was lost in thought, rather than being deliberately annoying.

"At any rate," he said, picking up as if he'd never paused, "I wanted you to consider human need as a criterion for initiating research." He cleared his throat. "Now, consider a completely different approach to our discussion. Suppose you could design a bomb capable of burning an entire city to the ground. Should one do so?"

"No!" she said, horrified. "You would never do that!"

"You are correct," the professor said. "I would not. There are some things that simply ought not be attempted, though reasonable men might argue that in the next war, the stakes will be much higher."

"The last war was fought to end wars."

"Let us set aside our disagreement in that matter and return to the question at hand. We are aware of the motivations and needs of—"

"Professor? What on earth are you talking about? What kind of project are you working on?"

"Communicating with the dead through scientific means."

The carriage rode on, bouncing on some ruts in the road.

"You are having fun at my expense," she whispered.

"Not at all. I'm quite serious. Before agreeing to assist me, I need you to consider the project, both as a problem of utility and as a possible transgression."

"Against God—"

"—and man," the professor said. "What we find might be as damaging as any bomb." He shifted again, looking straight ahead. "What would the people of New Concord do if it were revealed that God is a Methodist instead of a Presbyterian?"

Her laugh was involuntary. She covered her mouth with her hand.

"I'm asking if you care to assist me in this project. If you demur, I will find other tasks of a scientific nature for you, you needn't worry."

"You want my approval," she said, wonder in her voice.

"Yes. Now, suppose you lost a husband in the war?" he asked. "How would you feel about my project?"

She thought of Walter Raymond. What would she tell him, assuming she could tell him anything? That she'd been crushed when the telegram came? That she was better now, and hoped her happiness was what he wanted? That she thought of him most days, and likely would for the rest of her life? That the world was saved from future carnage by the war he died in? That his death had made a difference?

"I suppose," she said, "that I would embrace such a device. It's not possible, though. You can't talk to the dead."

He coughed into his fist, and said, his voice almost matter-of-fact, "I believe I've found a way. Tomorrow, we'll look at the groundwork of Misters Edison and Tesla." He turned to her. "Assuming, of course, that you agree to do so."

"I do." Even as she admitted this, a feeling of apprehension settled in her bones, cold as a winter night carriage ride.

CHAPTER TWELVE

First Snow/ The Edison Machines

Ohio, 1920

Eight inches of snow greeted them in the morning. Elizabeth made coffee and toasted bread. They sat together at the table watching the blizzard through the window. "You'd never have gotten here today in weather like this," Harry told her.

"If I'd made it, I'd be stuck here."

"Terrible fate, indeed," he joked.

"I'm going to clean up. You can make yourself useful by telling me what we're going to do in the workshop today."

Harry fetched the dishcloth from the sink basin and began wiping the table.

"I'll do that, Professor."

He ignored her. "Let's make quick work of your chores this morning."

"These are the chores you pay me to do," she said. "This isn't work for a gentleman."

He glanced at her, surprised. "My mother died when I was very young. I cooked and cleaned for my father. I even did laundry, though I was terrible at it. Keeping house is necessary work, and all work is noble. In fact, that's the only nobility I recognize."

"But you hired me to save you time." She seemed confounded by him.

Over the past two weeks, he had asked questions about her family and gotten an earful about her father. Perhaps home life had forever colored her opinion of men. "You will save me more time than before when we are in the workshop," he said. "As for household chores, you will still do the lion's share. But our specific roles are not chiseled in stone. They are in a state of transition."

She stood at the basin, one hand on her hip and a perplexed expression on her face. He could not help but find her adorable. "While we work," he continued, "I will fill you in on the efforts of Mr. Edison. We will be recreating his experiments in contacting the dead."

With this announcement, her demeanor changed. She focused on her chores while he talked, pausing only to ask an occasional question.

"As you well know from picking up my postal deliveries, I correspond with a number of researchers and inventors around the world. Scientists are, in truth, building on the efforts of each other, and the free exchange of ideas—and missteps—facilitates that. As it happens, I correspond with someone in Edison's Menlo Park facility." He paused to scrub at the breakfast flatware. "This may be steel, but it is hardly stainless," he muttered.

"What did the correspondence tell you about Edison's work?

"Edison believes that life is indestructible. He believes, to paraphrase his hypothesis, that souls, or essential personalities, are made of particles, much as substances are made of atoms. These particles of personality—a residue of thoughts and memories—could collect and manifest in what he calls *swarms*. If so, then a device might register their presence, or even amplify their attempts at communication. This is all quite reasonable. You are familiar with the dictum that energy can neither be created nor destroyed. What is a soul, if not pure energy?"

Elizabeth paused in her sweeping. "Is that all? Were there plans or drawings?"

"Actually, Edison tested a device last month. I received a description of the machine and have been recreating the experiment here."

"Does it work? Can you hear the dead?"

Harry answered from the back room where he was putting his bedding back in order. "There is no audio component to Edison's first trial run. I'll show you in a moment." He stood up, glancing around his room. "It's cold in here," he said. "How was your bed, by the way? I'm glad it was delivered before the storm. You might have had to wait another week."

"The bed is fine," she said. "Most comfortable. And I was pleased not to worry about you sleeping in a chair or on the floor."

Harry stepped into the main room again, rubbing his hands together. "I told you before. I don't require much sleep. Shall we go into the workshop? I am anxious to show you Edison's machine."

"Give me five minutes," Elizabeth said.

"Five," he said. "No more."

When she arrived in the workshop twenty minutes later, he handed her a bound journal. There were no entries. "I purchased a fresh volume for your notes. You will, of course, make date and time entries for any of our procedures?"

"Of course," she said. "Why a fresh journal?"

"The old volume had personal notes as well as notes on my research. We are establishing a more rigid protocol. Verification, Elizabeth." He smiled. "While you were busy evicting every last dust mote from our cottage, I set up Mr. Edison's first device on the long bench. Shall we?"

Elizabeth was already moving to the far back wall. She touched the prototypes, examining each one in turn. Tesla's model was a cluster of wires in a fruit jar sitting next to a pair of coil antennae. A second device looked vaguely like a cross between a phonograph and a cylindrical recorder. The shelves were otherwise full of electrical parts and pieces. "What are these machines?" she asked.

"Over here," he said, pointing to the Ritchie photometer. A box wired to a battery apparatus sat three feet from the photometer. A small lens faced the photometer.

Elizabeth pointed at the ceiling. "Why do you have electric lighting in the workshop, but nowhere else?"

"We're on the fringe of town, far from any power source. And the cottage is old. When I purchased this place, I wired the workroom myself using DC power. The wind charger is on the roof."

"The windmill?"

"Smaller than most mills, I think. There's a generator near the top. Batteries are in the closet." He pointed at a door near the rear of the room. "I use nickel-iron batteries from the Edison company. Quite useful. They can't be harmed by running them down or overcharging."

"There were no windows in this room," he continued, "which is why, when we turn off the lights, we will have an effective recreation of Edison's experiment." Harry moved the battery-wired box, directing it toward the photometer. "According to my friend, Edison pointed a pencil-thin beam of light at a photocell, which generated a measurable current. Fluctuations in the current would indicate an interruption of the beam."

He looked up. "The measurement of current notes interruptions. The photometer will measure *fluctuations*. I'm making it easier for spirits to communicate."

"Thomas Edison did this."

"Yes. Apparently, he had an audience of notable scientists as witnesses."

"Did it work?"

"No," Harry said. "I have tried several iterations of this experiment. The photocell was unsatisfactory, so I tried the photometer." He paused. "Part of the problem is the light source. A beam of light must, by necessity, diffuse and disperse over distance. A truly focused beam would have a better chance of success. I've toyed with the idea of a collimated beam—"

"I'm not familiar with the word."

"The term comes from a misreading of a Latin word. No matter." His voice sped up, and he waved his hands as he spoke. "It refers to light traveling in parallel lines. I could focus this beam with lenses, you see, but it would be focused on a single point. More useful to have a tight, parallel beam that can be interrupted at any point along the length."

Elizabeth stared at the apparatus. "Are you going to test the machine now?"

"Certainly. Turn off the light."

Elizabeth located the light switch near the door. "Are you ready?"

Harry flipped the light box on and said, "Go ahead."

The dying filament of the overhead bulb left the light beam as the only source of light in the room. "What now?" she asked. The beam cast shadows across the room.

Harry cleared his throat. "If there are any spirits in the room, feel free to announce your presence by interrupting the beam." The beam went undisturbed, but from across the room, he heard an odd sound coming from Elizabeth. Was she laughing?

After five minutes, during which Harry repeated his invitation without the appearance of any spirits, Elizabeth turned on the lights. "May I ask you something?"

"Certainly," he said.

"If the beam had been interrupted, how would we proceed? One interruption for yes, and two for no?"

"I hadn't considered it, but I suppose so."

"How is Mr. Edison's machine different from Madame Phoenix's spirit rapping?"

Harry bit his lower lip, his brow furrowed in thought. "I suppose there's no real difference, is there?"

"He expects spirits to come rapping, tapping on our chamber door?"

"But Thomas Edison—"

"Nevermore," Elizabeth said, smiling prettily.

•   •   •   •   •

"A second Edison attempt apparently involves a sort of valve. As my friend relates, Edison uses the term valve in a thermionic sense—the emission of electrons from a heated substance."

"As in a Fleming valve?" she asked.

Harry stopped to smile and shake his head. "I must constantly adjust my estimation of you. You are quite brilliant."

Elizabeth blushed. "Finish your account, please."

"I've made you uncomfortable."

"I am unused to compliments."

Harry turned away. "Well, then. Edison used a fluted horn, like the cone in a phonograph. The horn contains a valve. Both the horn and valve were meant to amplify sound so that a microphone can pick up and record amplified vibrations."

Elizabeth pointed at the shelf in the rear of the shop. "Is that Mr. Edison's second machine?"

"I have no idea how it compares to Mr. Edison's prototypes, though it's meant to do so. My friend did not have access to either a model or a schematic. He could not be sure that Edison even built a prototype. He did mention the use of potassium permanganate."

"What on earth for?" she asked.

Harry shrugged. "To enhance conduction? The effort in the design, such as I understand it, aims to increase the sensitivity of the device."

Elizabeth put a finger to her chin. She'd crossed the room to the second machine, staring at it. "He's imagined that spirit voices are too faint for the human ear, hasn't he? He's trying to enhance audible sound in order to test his hypothesis."

"It's a common approach," Harry said. "Imagine a phenomenon, and then devise a test to prove its existence. Mathematicians postulated the Schwarzschild radius— the point at which a mass becomes a singularity. Astronomers immediately began searching for physical evidence."

"Have they found anything?"

"No. I think the limitations of telescope optics inhibit any such verification."

Elizabeth touched the device, running a slender finger over the curve of the instrument's horn. "I assume that the limits of auditory instrumentation prevent a successful test of Mr. Edison's device?"

"My device. Don't blame Mr. Edison. And yes, the test was unsuccessful." He pointed at the cylinder recorder attached to the horn. "I've picked up a few sounds, but nothing of definitive substance."

"Which means either that the device is insufficient, or that there are no spirit voices to be received."

"In a nutshell," he said. He watched her caress the device, running a fingertip over the fluted horn. *Good God,* he thought. *To be that machine, if only for a moment.*

"Are we to run another test?" she asked.

"Yes," he said. "Several tests. And you will record all of our efforts."

"May I sit at the smaller table? I can write there."

"Of course. Use a chair from the other room." Harry bit his lower lip. Many amenities were missing in the cottage. If she had a stool or tall chair, the task of recording as he worked would be simple. He himself never sat in the lab. Rather, he'd record his notes at the end of the day, seated at the table in the main room.

His notes. She must never see them. He'd written about her, of course. Now, his enterprises had a partner, and some distance was required.

During the second trial run of the speaker and recorder device, an odd, unidentifiable sound etched into the celluloid cylinder. Harry replayed it several times. "Any ideas?" he asked her. "It sounds like breathing."

"That's how it sounds to me."

She wore an odd smile, and when she tilted her head, he had to ask her, "What are you going on about?"

She laughed, the breathy sound of a flute. "I believe it recorded your own breathing, professor."

"Good God," Harry said. "We should save the cylinder then. We'll sell it when we become famous."

•　　•　　•　　•　　•

Supper consisted of roast chicken, a muffin, and a salad. Elizabeth left the workshop early—with some reluctance— and set about preparing dinner while the professor straightened up the benches and shelves. When he joined her, he prepared the salad. She frowned at the produce. The vegetables were in their dotage and barely edible. She wished for an icebox, but she would not tell him so. He'd already bought her a bed and bureau, stocked the pantry, added several cooking utensils, and added to her sparse wardrobe. He'd done so without a hint of reluctance. By contrast, her mother regarded any purchase as a perpetual regret. Elizabeth could not help but anticipate the professor would eventually feel the same. He would realize what a bother she was—

But not in the workshop. There, she'd held her own, much to her pride and pleasure. The day had been better than any daydream she'd imagined as a young girl. She hadn't bumbled anything, and the professor seemed lifted by her presence. Less like the dour employer and more like the happy gentleman who'd escorted her home each night.

Home. This was her home now, in a way. She was still an employee, but a respected one. Her prospects were infinitely better than they'd been just a few weeks ago.

Tomorrow, they would turn to Mr. Tesla's device. The professor had assured her that Tesla's approach was completely different than Edison's. She did not think much of Edison's machines. His basic assumption— spirits lingered and longed to speak to us but required various signaling and amplification—seemed flawed. What would Tesla's approach be?

After supper, the professor reviewed her notes without comment. He sat at the table, chin propped in his hand, reading and rereading.

"Are you unhappy with my notes?" she asked finally.

"No, not at all," he said. "You are precise and thorough." He frowned. "I see that you've added some personal commentary. Your ideas—"

"I'm sorry!' she said. She'd been so instantly comfortable in the workshop, she hadn't hesitated to add her opinions, mostly about Edison's assumptions. It seemed to her that the rapid advancement of technology made it seem as if science could do anything. That was, in her opinion, an illusion. Mr. Edison may well be a genius, but he presumed much. "I was carried away with the day, Professor. I won't do that again."

He blinked. "Nonsense," he said. "Your views may well be the anchor that keep me from flying off into fancy. We are partners in a joint venture. Your opinions will always be welcome. Particularly any disagreements. Working alone, I've had no such input." He took another bite of chicken.

Elizabeth sat still. Under the table, her hands fluttered in a joyous dance.

Chapter Thirteen

Spirit Radio/Into the Vortex

Ohio, 1920

The first day of the storm had been like an adventure, but by the second day, a cold melancholy settled over the cottage. Harry gazed at the sky through his window. Wind blew snow from drift to drift, erasing the horizon with a blurred swatch of white. Trees hunched like old men, covered in shawls of snow. Inside, a small fire battled the cold. Just as moisture seeps into cracks, freezing and breaking the sturdiest cement, the damp air worked its way into his bones, breaking him and leaving him weak.

Elizabeth busied herself at the sink. He studied her from behind, wondering what she thought of his silence. He was not a stranger to bouts of depression. He'd battled such lapses at regular intervals, beginning with Drew's death. But since Elizabeth's arrival, he'd avoided the feeling of despair that derailed his work and left him useless. Now, he had to acknowledge that she was not the panacea he'd hoped for.

In France, they'd treated his malady with a combination of baths, massage, and suspicion. In Harry's case, the diagnosis of shell shock coincided with the actual burst of a shell, in keeping with the belief that the concussion of explosives caused organic trauma. His shock was thought to be "commotional." Microhemorrhaging in the brain, rather than psychological damage. The burns on his leg lent credence to the belief—they were physical and could be treated conventionally.

As with other victims, underlying doubts about his courage ensured that his stay was unpleasant. Harry was an American, presumed unable to speak French, though he understood what was said about him perfectly. They suspected that he was *faux malade.* The tremors, the physical reaction to the sound of shells, and the long periods of silence were regarded with misgiving. If not for the burns on his leg, he would have been returned to the front.

On one occasion, the doctors implemented the electric cure—a painful dose of electric shock meant both as treatment and as discipline. Harry refused a second treatment. By then, the Armistice had been declared, and Harry found himself homeward bound.

The tremors disappeared upon his return to New Concord. His terror of thunder continued. Harry chose to confront his fears directly, forcing himself to sit on the porch during lightning storms, fingers dug into his thighs. The fear did not abate, nor did the occasional sense of lost time or bouts of depression.

"Will we go into the workshop now?" Elizabeth asked. Her voice dragged him back into the cold room, but he was unable to answer her for a moment. "Are you well?" she asked.

He shook his head as if to clear it, knowing full well that he would not be able to spill the illness from his head like salt from a shaker. "I'm not hitting on all sixes today," he said. "We'll work, but the mood may suffer."

She nodded.

"We should clean up first," he suggested.

"The work is done, Professor."

He glanced around. Indeed, she'd managed to clean the breakfast dishes, sweep the floors, and otherwise tidy the place without his notice. He sank in his chair. *She must think me mad,* he thought.

"We can wait until the afternoon, Professor."

"Harry," he said. The word came out surlier than he'd intended.

Elizabeth tilted her head, meeting his gaze.

"Call me Harry, please. I have not been a professor since before the war." He took a deep breath. "On occasion, I lecture at the college, but that owes more to the generosity of the faculty than anything I offer the students."

"I'm quite certain you're wrong," Elizabeth said. "I loved your lectures."

Harry tapped the table with his fingertips to give his hand something to do. Elizabeth sat down across from him, her hands folded in her lap. He said, "I sound ungrateful. I do enjoy the contact." He met her gaze. "But I really would prefer you called me Harry."

"All right," she said. "Harry."

"This mood of mine." He closed his eyes. "This is another manifestation of my wartime experience." The words crawled out of him. "Your chosen employer cannot be counted on for pleasant company."

He expected her to deny the claim or try to cheer him. She did neither. Instead, she gave him a smile and left the room. This gave him a jolt of surprise. He hadn't the energy to fend off her questions. The realization that he would not have to do so gave him a modicum of peace.

Later, when he realized that he was still sitting at the table, he looked up to find her cleaning the pantry cupboard. "Can you finish that later?" he asked.

"Of course."

"Let's go into the workshop, then." He managed to force himself through the workshop door and across the room, retrieving what appeared to be a canning jar stuffed with wires. He set the contraption on the long bench, fixing the wire ends to a small speaker. Next, he attached two coiled copper antennae. 'This is Mr. Tesla's device," he said. "The only modification I've made involves the electron relay." He tapped a small box. "A triode vacuum tube amplifies the signal. This is the only part of the device that requires power. The Tesla device itself works without power."

He turned the amplifier on to a squawking sound, followed by the low hum of static. Next, he attached the Tesla jar and stepped back. The sounds began immediately.

Elizabeth's eyes were wide with surprise. Perhaps fear.

The speaker produced voices. Snippets of words, distant and tinny, spoken in an unknown language. He let the demonstration continue for more than five minutes. As always, there were words he thought he could understand. The French word *fleur*. The German word *bisschen*. A few words in English. Background noise and distortion from the amplifier interfered with any clear delineation of the sounds. The vocal pitch changed briefly, as if the gender of the speaker had changed.

"What are we listening to?" Elizabeth asked.

Harry turned off the amplifier. "Inductor capacitor circuits. When Tesla heard this, he thought he might have been contacting the dead. That, or contacting an alien species from outer space."

"You are joking."

Harry shook his head. "The device picks up electromagnetic waves. I have no idea of the source. Waves seem to be everywhere in the modern world."

"I heard words," Elizabeth said. "I don't think all of them were in English."

Harry asked, "Did you hear words, or did your mind assign form to the sounds you heard?"

"I couldn't be sure," Elizabeth said. "Have you tried recording these sounds? You have the cylinder recorder."

Harry nodded, smiling. "Good, good. Yes, I recorded the sounds. They are considerably less convincing in recorded form. I had difficulty locating words I thought I'd identified. That might be due to the quality of the recording. Or it might be an indication that I was assigning meaning to random sounds."

Elizabeth walked to the smaller bench and opened the journal. "Give me a moment, please." She pointed at the fruit jar. "Can you bring that over here?" Harry unhooked the jar from the speaker and vacuum tube amplifier. When he deposited the Tesla device on the smaller table, Elizabeth pointed to one of the internal elements. "What is this?" she asked.

When her questions were answered, Harry returned everything to the back shelves, careful with each component.

He'd introduced his new assistant to the problem, both as an exploration of need and a discussion of propriety. He'd demonstrated the attempts of Edison and Tesla. The final step would be to explain his approach and show her his prototype. Elizabeth would need an explanation of the theoretical math, but she was quick and capable.

She stood at the small bench, bent over her journal. Her slender figure was arresting. The thought gave him pause, not because he found her fetching—he did—but because the shroud of depression that darkened the day had lifted noticeably.

•   •   •   •   •

Harry sat at the table, eating baked pork chops and carrot muffins while pouring over Elizabeth's notes. As part of her entry, she'd drawn a careful diagram of the Tesla jar. "Your drawing is meticulous," he said.

Elizabeth sat at the table, her food for the most part untouched. "Thank you."

Harry regarded the drawing. "As electrical devices become more prevalent, more complex, schemata like this will be necessary." He looked up. "Where did you learn this?"

"From you," she said. "You showed us radio drawings in class. They were beautiful, like art. Only useful. I am a fair hand with a pen and ink, so I followed up in the library at Muskingum."

"Time well spent," Harry said. "Now, tell me what's wrong."

Elizabeth turned away. "It's nothing, Professor."

"Harry."

Elizabeth's shoulders trembled. "It's something apart from our work."

Harry waited. Something was distressing Elizabeth. He hoped he was not the cause of her unease.

"This may well strike you as ridiculous. But I am worried about my parents. It's winter, and my father does not work. My mother sews, but that may not get them through the season. They were getting the larger portion of my salary, and I think they counted on it."

Harry nodded. "What should be done?"

Elizabeth seemed uneasy. "You mentioned that I would be in line for a wage increase. I want them to receive money each week."

"Not all," he advised. "You must keep money for yourself. For your future." The words held a special irony for him that he tried not to show in his expression.

"I don't want to see them," she continued. "Not for a long time. I wondered how to impose on you to see the funds delivered."

"Don't give that a second thought," Harry said. "How much a week should they receive?"

Elizabeth explained the sum she had in mind. "You think I'm foolish."

Harry closed his eyes. "Of course not," he said. "I have my place in the world through the generosity of the same man who sponsored you at Muskingum. Our baker friend gifts me loaves, like the fisherman of Galilee. Madame Phoenix buys ginger cookies with my patronage. The widow Hartley benefits from our pantry fund. The world is a better place for acts of kindness, big or small." He leaned forward. "A good heart is never foolish." He frowned. "But put all that aside. We have work to do." He walked into his bedroom, returning with some pages that had been cut from his old journal. "Study these equations, please. Tomorrow, we'll look at the device I've been testing."

Elizabeth spread the sheets out on the table and began to read while Harry cleaned the dinner dishes. After a great deal of time, Elizabeth asked, "Can electric power be generated by the earth's electromagnetic field?"

Harry shrugged. "I don't believe so. Tesla did. That much is certain. He built a tower on Long Island in New York toward that purpose. The idea was to use high-voltage radio-frequency energy with a Tesla coil. I have a smaller model of his coil in the workshop. At any rate, the Long Island power transmitter is connected to a deep electrical ground. Tesla thought he could force low-voltage oscillations from the earth's capacitance—shake loose the

Earth's power potential. By using a receiving coil, that energy would provide free power."

Elizabeth said, "And?"

Harry shrugged again. "It didn't work. That, or the project was never finished. However—"

"Your device."

"Yes. Tesla's understanding of the electromagnetic field spurred an idea. That, and his device. Let me ask you something. Suppose that you were a creature of only two dimensions—not three."

Elizabeth frowned.

"How would I communicate with you? How would I even perceive you? Should you turn sideways, you would disappear." He laughed. She did not. "More importantly, how would I describe the third dimension to you?"

"I don't know. Try to imagine a third dimension as—" She sighed. "I don't know."

"Now, my three-dimensional assistant, how can we imagine a fourth dimension?"

Elizabeth stood, walked to the sink, and began toweling the dishes and putting them away. Harry had washed. "I am having trouble imagining such a thing."

"Not surprising," Harry said. "Math is our best friend in the matter." He sat at the table, pointing at two of the papers spread out on the table. "Just as mathematicians postulate collapsed stars and astronomers search the skies for them, I theorized the shape of an electromagnetic field in a fourth dimension and set about designing a device that made use of the results."

Elizabeth stood with her back to him, opening and closing cupboard doors.

"In the fourth dimension, an electromagnetic field has two components—the potential and the vortex. You know what a vortex is, do you not?"

"Like a tornado. Like a whirlpool."

"Yes!" Harry said, with some enthusiasm. "My idea is to approach an electromagnetic field, not as a grid, but as a vortex. Think of it as an extra dial on a radio."

Elizabeth stood still, her hands on the sink.

"Now, here is something that will amuse you, given our experiences with Madame Phoenix," he continued. "Mediums speak of *spiritual vortexes*—intersecting ley lines in the earth's energy grid. Those intersections are regarded as spiritual hot spots, where psychic communication can occur. Such places can occasionally be spotted by anomalies in plant life, such as two entirely different species of tree growing together as a single entity." He laughed. "Perhaps the spiritualists know something after all."

She turned to face him with the glint of tears in her eyes. "I'm sorry, Professor—Harry. I don't understand the mathematics." She gritted her teeth for a moment. "I may not be smart enough to assist you."

Harry gripped the arm of his chair, lest he rush over and wrap his arms around her. "You do yourself an injustice."

She sat down across the table from him, wiping her eyes. "I read your papers. I have no idea what they mean. In the world of theoretical electricity . . . I am insulation. I make a poor conductor."

Harry sat back and took a deep breath. What came to mind was the memory of Mr. Brympton, questioning him about Plato's Socrates, and the secret smile Harry had taken as Brympton's amusement. Now, he knew better. The old man's smile was one of pride.

"My father and I moved to Mr. Brympton's estate when I was seven," Harry said. "I had daily access to one of the finest private libraries imaginable. When I exhausted that excellent resource, I transferred my efforts to the college library. And you?" He chose his words carefully, lest he insult her. "You cared for your parents."

Elizabeth slumped in her chair. She looked downcast.

"I am at least seven years older than you. Having had the luxury of more than two decades of study—"

"Minus the war."

Harry raised a finger, as if scoring a point. "That was a laboratory of a different nature. Still, I've had a life filled with study. So, you are behind me in this matter. This is the state of things as they are. But you are already indispensable to me, and the remainder of your life can be spent catching up. I suspect you will do so." He stood. "We can wring our hands and curse society's prejudices, or we can get to work. What is your choice?"

"You've become a stunt-and-cheer coach," Elizabeth said.

"Never did the Muskingum football team any good," Harry said. "Perhaps if they'd allowed women cheerleaders."

"Someday." Elizabeth grabbed the papers from the table and stacked them. "My journal depictions of your device will not include schemata. I will satisfy myself with artistic renderings."

"For now," Harry said.

CHAPTER FOURTEEN

Digging a Grave/A Grave Miscalculation

Ohio, 1920

The trick, Harry explained, was to find a sympathetic frequency. Otherwise, the speaker would transmit static and other random noises. What frequency? He did not know.

The machine consisted, in part, of a series of unconventional electromagnets—odd iron shapes wrapped in copper wire. His device was in a state of constant evolution as Harry configured and reconfigured his magnetic field. Mr. Ashby, the hardware store owner, would be able to put a new roof on his house given the amount of copper wire and custom iron shapes Harry had purchased.

Elizabeth, with the deft hands of an artist, wrapped the iron shapes in wire, fashioning tight rows of copper with a precision that surely put her mother's sewing and knitting to shame. Harry immediately recognized the superiority of her efforts and tasked her with redoing his own good-intentioned work. Elizabeth sat at the smaller table on her new shop stool, carefully winding and spooling while Harry tried different arrangements of his new components, aided by his latest set of baffling equations.

Elizabeth punctuated the silence with an occasional question. "Suppose the machine works," she said. "Will we have to learn other languages to communicate?"

"*Bonjour la personne décédée,*" Harry said. Elizabeth gave him a blank look. "Hello dead person," he explained.

After another ten minutes of silence, he added, "I expect that if the spirit survives as energy in another dimension, they will still have some proximity to this one."

"The way ghosts haunt the places they died," Elizabeth mused. Her voice betrayed her skepticism.

"Why not? 'Tis the season of ghosts."

Christmas Eve was a day away.

Harry had asked Elizabeth to attend services with him at the Presbyterian church the following evening. When he'd lived with Mr. Brympton, his attendance was required. Once the war ended, his visits became irregular. "I am due to make an appearance." New Concord was a small town, a deeply spiritual town, and certain things were expected.

With the occasion in mind, Harry purchased a new dress for Elizabeth, and along with it, a new hat. She explained that the church required women to wear head coverings, though men wore none. The distinction was meant to remind worshipers of the subordination of women to men. Harry had noticed the hats, of course, accepting the custom without understanding it. Now, he listened without comment and bought her a pretty hat— silently deciding that this visit might also be his last. If Elizabeth wished to return to the fold, she had his blessing, along with the requisite hat.

On their most recent trip to New Concord, they'd purchased a fat hen for Christmas dinner—a turkey was too much food for two—along with parsnips, potatoes, and apples for the stuffing. Elizabeth had prepared the plum pudding weeks earlier. On his own, Harry purchased a small jar of moonshine from Mrs. Hartley, and though

Harry was not a drinking man, the thought of a minor legal infraction on Christmas Day seemed delicious.

In the workshop, Harry watched Elizabeth wind copper wire around an iron horseshoe, concentrating as if the exact rows would be the sole determinant of her fate in the world. Her singular focus allowed him to study her without regard to propriety. Her features seemed remarkably proportioned, though a close eye revealed that her forehead was slightly larger and her ears slightly smaller than average. She wore her hair tied up and back, ignoring these deviations from perfection. The overall effect was to emphasize her eyes—those maddeningly expressive eyes.

She glanced up at him, and he looked away. "I've spoken to your parents, as you requested," he said, at a loss for what else to say.

Her expression softened. A downturn of the corners of her mouth. A sadness in those dark brown eyes. "Did they conduct themselves well?" The question sounded rhetorical.

"Your father argued for a lump sum, as if I were there to buy your freedom and installment payments were inappropriate."

Elizabeth's face reddened.

"You are not responsible for your parents' comportment," Harry said. "And they are no reflection on you. You are quite your own person. The mystery of how you survived to become someone of quality rivals the mystery of what those two people saw in each other. I detected no affection between them."

"I do not recall seeing anything of the sort growing up," Elizabeth admitted.

"Perhaps they are that unhappy couple that lives to torment each other." Harry rushed ahead, eager to have a conversation.

"When my grandmother was still alive, Mother and I would visit. The two of them would sit at the table and talk about my father. About what a disappointment he was."

"I see. Your father is a very large man."

"Yes. He intends to dig a grave with his teeth."

Harry stopped short. Elizabeth's face held a hint of anger. For her father or for himself? "He's a genial sort, though."

"Yes. Alcohol mellows him and makes him colorful. I learned a great many phrases from him."

"What kind of phrases?" Harry asked.

Elizabeth frowned, blushing. "Like . . . getaway sticks?"

Harry laughed. "What are getaway sticks?"

"Legs."

Harry tried not to laugh. "What of Constance Rose?"

"She is even less pleasant," Elizabeth finished, her tone sharp now. "But her sewing kept the pantry stocked."

Harry noted her pained expression and changed his tone immediately. "To their credit, they kept their vows. For better or worse. In the absence of better, they weathered the worse well enough to raise you. And you are surely their finest accomplishment."

Elizabeth blushed a shade of red that did honor to her family name. Rising to go, she said, "Excuse me, please" and left the room.

I went too far, he thought. *I am eternally clumsy in these matters*. He looked at the unfinished electromagnet on Elizabeth's short bench. He could not continue with his tinkering until the wire wrapping was complete. He gave himself a disgusted sigh. She would busy herself at the sink until everything in the house was perfect. Perhaps she would use the bathroom. Finally, she would hide in her room until morning. If he gave her ten more minutes, she could finish the evening without further discomfort from him.

Just two days until Christmas. It was customary to exchange gifts before Christmas dinner. He had two presents for her. One was a trifle. Having already purchased her black dress in Zanesville, her proportions were known to the dressmaker. He'd asked for fashion advice and then ignored it, opting for a floor-length red velvet evening dress with a V-neck. Luckily, he had the visit to Madame Phoenix to explain the first dress and Christmas to explain the second.

As for the second gift, he might never give it to her. He'd purchased the ring anyway, more a whim than thoughtful preparation for a happy outcome. White gold and platinum with a tiny emerald-cut diamond and a sapphire accent stone, the ring was an extravagance that both shamed and excited him. He had always been a frugal man. After this, he promised himself, he would keep tighter strings on his inheritance.

• • •

On Christmas Eve, the weather relented. Snow still drifted down from overcast skies, but the wind was gone, and the temperature had risen enough to offer a respite from the typical cold that gripped Ohio in December. Elizabeth stepped outside several times to take in the still, fresh air—a chilly tonic. She could almost believe that spring was coming soon, instead of two more months of hard winter.

When Harry suggested they go for an afternoon walk, she jumped at the chance. Rather than walk toward town, they took the road west, parallel to the old National Road, following the wheel ruts from cars and carriages. "We won't go far," Harry promised. Elizabeth didn't care how far they went. She'd missed their walks.

The cream-colored sun gave the threadbare trees a soft coat of light. He walked next to her, so close that she might have taken his hand. He smiled at her. Elizabeth smiled back. Snowflakes caught in his eyelashes, and he brushed them away with a laugh.

On the other side of a hill, Harry left the road, climbing a gentle slope to a copse of beech trees, striking against the winter sky with their smooth, steel-gray bark. Here they found an unlikely splash of color. Winterberry shrubs, stripped of their leaves, were ornamented with red and gold berries. The yellow, red, and orange tendrils of witch hazel stood out against the snow. Harry moved through the trees, past a blue spruce to a tiny pocket of white flowers with dark green stems. "*Helleborus niger*," he said, squatting down. "The Christmas rose."

Winter or not, Elizabeth felt her face grow hot.

Harry reached out and touched the flowers with his fingertips. "According to legend, a young girl visited the Christ child in Bethlehem. She had no gift to offer, which left her weeping. Flowers sprouted where her teardrops fell." He gestured at Elizabeth with an outstretched hand, and then at the flowers. "Elizabeth Rose, meet the other Christmas rose."

"They're beautiful," Elizabeth said.

"Yes, they are," he answered.

•   •   •   •   •

Harry hired the carriage driver to transport them to the church that evening. Elizabeth put on her new dress and hat. "You look very nice," Harry said, thinking that the dress was somewhat plain. He'd rather have seen her in the red velvet dress he'd bought, though perhaps red velvet wasn't an appropriate look for church.

On the road, he noticed that she shivered in her thin coat. "We're going to have to buy you a better coat."

She leaned against him. "I'm fine, Harry."

When the carriage reached the church, there was enough light to see her face. Her eyes, an unmistakable litmus test of her mood, were iridescent. Her smile was a bright sliver of moon. He offered his arm and she took it. "Merry Christmas," she whispered.

The church spire rose above the entrance like three boxes stacked on top of each other, each one smaller than the one below it. The pointed roof over the bell tower looked like a woman's cap. The rest of the building was a plain white rectangle, cut by tall lancet windows on the sides.

Stepping through the huge wooden doors, Harry saw Elizabeth's parents. The Roses sat in the very last pew on the right aisle, eyeing everyone who entered. Seeing Elizabeth and Harry made them flinch.

The pews were arranged in three columns—the largest being in the middle, with smaller rows of plain benches on the right and left. Some members of the community gathered in groups, exchanging wishes for the holiday. Others, particularly those in the front, center pews, sat quietly, waiting for the prayers, music, the reading, the sermon, and the Sacraments to begin. Harry recalled his days in church with Mr. Brympton. People entered and sat with solemn faces, waiting until after the service to congregate outside. But it was cold outside, and this was Christmas Eve.

Their arrival sparked some notice. The widow Hartley made her way from an aisle seat in the pews, one hand clutching a lace handkerchief. "Hello, Professor!" she said, her vocal pitch somewhat higher than when she greeted Elizabeth.

"I wondered if you would be here this evening," Harry said. Elizabeth stepped away, glancing back at her parents. To his knowledge, she'd had no contact with them since moving to Harry's cottage. Her face had gone blank.

"Very kind of you to transport Miss Rose in your carriage," the widow said. "It's a cold, dark walk from your cottage out in the wilderness."

Harry glanced away. "It's wonderful to see so many people from the community out on this winter's evening."

"Of course," she said. "It's the eve of the birth of our Lord." Her tone had no hint of her usual bluster, which brought a smile to his face.

One group of churchgoers had stopped talking and were turned to face him. A couple passed behind him. He heard the woman say, "pleasure-mad daughters," as if she were relating a story from a confession magazine. He wouldn't have given it a second thought, but when one of the women from yet another group glared at him, he began to form a different impression.

"Professor?"

He looked down at the widow, who gazed up at him with a knowing expression. To his right, Elizabeth stood near her mother, who stared straight ahead, her lips barely moving.

"We're a small town," the widow said. "Not everyone is as open-minded as myself." She leaned in closer, as if in confidence. "The town doesn't blame you, Professor. Women are the guardians of morality. Young girls are expected to behave as if made of finer stuff."

"But men—"

"Men are men," she said firmly. "I was married for many years, as you know, and the behavior of men is no mystery to me."

"Fascinating," Harry said. He directed his attention to Elizabeth. Her father turned away from her, facing the wall to his right. Elizabeth's expression wilted.

"She's his housekeeper." Another voice from behind.

Harry glanced to the front. The pastor made his way to the altar. People began drifting toward their seats.

"I believe," he said in a low voice, "that I've made a terrible miscalculation."

Mrs. Hartley tilted her head. "Professor?"

"I may have given people the wrong impression."

"Oh," Mrs. Hartley said. "I think I understand. Well, don't blame yourself. If there's a misunderstanding, her parents own the lion's share of the blame."

Elizabeth made her way back to him, eyes bright with tears. At first, she would not meet his gaze. When he took her arm, hoping to direct her to a seat in the center pew, she said, "I'm sorry. I don't feel well. Would you be disappointed if we left?"

He turned back to the widow Hartley, bowed, wished her a Merry Christmas, and headed for the back door. He resisted the urge to cast a furious glance at Elizabeth's mother, striding past her instead. At the door, he bumped into Mr. Albanesi, the baker, along with his round little wife. "Professor! So nice to see you here!"

Harry stopped to shake the baker's hand and greet his wife. Elizabeth tried to slip around them but couldn't. "Are you leaving?" Albanesi asked. "The service is just beginning!"

"We ran late ourselves," Mrs. Albanesi confided, her voice breathy and excited. "So much business before the holiday! But we're here now, and you must sit with us!"

"So sorry," Harry said. Elizabeth had managed to circumnavigate the baker's wife and push her way through the door. Harry mumbled a few more apologies and rushed out into the night. He found Elizabeth alone in the carriage. The driver was inside the church, listening to the opening prayer.

CHAPTER FIFTEEN

The Long Ride Home/Christmas Day

Ohio, 1920

In Harry's estimation, the ride back to his cottage took the better part of a century. The sky was clear and pocked with stars, but in the absence of clouds, the temperature plummeted. He'd meant to bring blankets. In his haste to attend the evening service, he'd forgotten them. Elizabeth's poor coat was not enough to keep her warm. Even Harry, usually too preoccupied to notice the weather, sat shivering in his seat.

Elizabeth did not speak the entire ride. Halfway home, he asked her if she were comfortable. She didn't answer, and he did not press. The question was absurd.

His burned leg trembled. Sometimes the nerve in his thigh began to fire, and the only thing to bring relief was a long walk to loosen the tissue. He considered asking the driver to pull over and let him out so he could walk home, but decided against it. Elizabeth might take offense, or worse, blame herself for his exit.

The widow Hartley's words came back to him as a taunt. "We're a small town." What had he been thinking? He'd walked in with his housekeeper on his arm as if she were a fine watch. *Look what I have here.*

The carriage struck a rock that had been buried under the snow, and Harry's leg shot out, a bolt of pain shooting up his hip. He grimaced and bit his lower lip.

The trees to either side of the carriage stooped in the dark as if to snatch them. For the first time in years, he thought of a shadow on the bedroom wall, back in his youth. He'd mistaken the shadow for his mother, come back from the dead to drag him to the underworld. Now, the low branches of the trees reached in the dark with spindle fingers of dead wood. He glared at the dark shapes and cursed them silently.

Finally, the carriage delivered them to the cottage. Harry dealt with the driver while Elizabeth rushed inside. By the time Harry entered, she was in her room, door closed. He took a seat at the table, hoping she would eventually join him. He would say whatever was necessary to make her feel better. An explanation. An apology.

She stayed in her room. He could hear no sound. He might as well have been alone.

·　　·　　·　　·　　·

Unable to sleep, Harry visited his workshop. He gazed sadly at the unfinished electromagnet and wondered for the first time if she might decide against continuing in his employ. She'd left her parents. She might well leave him. Between documentation, magnet wiring, and her observations, he'd come to depend on her.

His machine lay on the long bench. He ran his hand along the components, wishing the contraption worked. What he wouldn't give for a chance to ask advice of his father. Of Mr. Brympton. Or his mother, for that matter.

He also longed to speak to Drew and tell him all about this strange creature who'd become so important to him. Drew had been deeply in love with his wife. He'd have understood.

He turned the power on and positioned the microphone and speaker. He touched the tuner—a simple circuit with an inductor and a ceramic capacitor—and began changing the frequency. "Hello? Hello?" He spoke softly, not wanting to alert Elizabeth.

No answer. Of course. He frowned.

Of what difference could he boast between himself and poor Madame Phoenix? She had her beliefs. He had his. *Yes, but you'll allow no tricks in your workshop.* Here in the workshop, at least, he insisted upon the truth.

But was that so in all matters? Had he been totally honest with Elizabeth? In the beginning, he'd focused only on her role as his assistant, lest she doubt her abilities and his motives. But now? *One way or the other*, he decided, *I will tell her how I feel. She will make her decisions based on the facts. I owe her that.*

He adjusted the frequency on the device again.

"Hello?"

The speaker rebuked him with the steady hiss of static.

Morning brought another storm. Wind lashed the cottage, whistling in the eaves. Heat from the stove brought little relief from the cold. Elizabeth wore her coat indoors as she silently prepared the midday feast. Harry resolved not to prod, but his silence only deepened hers, as if the cold had frozen every molecule in the cottage.

When the hen was stuffed and placed in the oven, Elizabeth turned and said, "You will have your dinner at noon, sir."

Harry frowned. "You will dine with me?"

"No," she said. "I don't believe I'll be hungry."

"It's Christmas," he said. "You will dine with me." He was not used to issuing orders outside of the workshop. She regarded him without comment. Then she turned and began cleaning the dishes in the sink.

Frustrated, Harry issued a series of sighs, ranging from a sigh of disgust to a sigh of melancholy. Elizabeth moved into the bedrooms, cleaning one after the other.

Harry changed tactics. He retrieved the bottle of moonshine and poured a glass for each of them. Perhaps a small dose would ease the tension. When he called to her and offered her a glass, she reacted with dismay. "No thank you. My father drinks," she said. "He's a drunk."

Harry grabbed both glasses and the jar, pouring them all down the drain. Having done so, he turned back. "I'm not your father," he said.

Her confused expression told him he'd failed to make his point. Thinking on the matter, he decided that he had no idea what point he was trying to make. He sat back down at the table to wait.

At length, Elizabeth joined him, though she would not meet his gaze. "I spoke to my parents last night," she said. "It seems that all of New Concord thinks I am a gold digger and a skate-around." She said this with a matter-of-fact tone, but her lower lip trembled when she finished.

"You and I know that isn't true," Harry said. Truth was his final arbiter.

"People think I came here to work my way into your life."

"Who thinks that?" he asked, scoffing.

"Who *doesn't* think that?"

Harry bit the inside of his cheek. "You're the best person I know."

"I'm your housekeeper."

It was one thing to argue on her behalf. It was another entirely to argue *with* her, as if she were his opponent. "You stopped being a housekeeper some time ago."

"They see smoke and imagine a fire," she said.

The difficult thing about quarreling with her, he thought ruefully, was the very real possibility that, despite his logic and reasoning, he would lose the argument. "There's no fire. We know that."

"Yes," she said, looking away. "No fire at all. You are quite right."

"So, why would you care what people think?" he asked.

Her lips pressed into a thin line. Was she angry? "Because, for one thing, I'm not a *cooze*," she said, wincing as she finished.

The word shocked him. It was such a harsh expression—one he hadn't heard since the war. Worse, it came from her mouth, and worst of all, if that was what the community thought of her, then it was his fault. "Don't use that word. That word is on one side of the galaxy, and you are on the other." He bit his lip. "I will make this right. I'll talk to people in town."

Her nose crinkled and her mouth twisted. She might laugh. Or cry.

"I'm a war hero, remember?" he said. "A professor at Muskingum. They will listen to me."

She put her elbows on the table and propped her chin in her hands. "Suppose someone approached you with a story about how he'd never . . ." She paused before finishing. "Never *hauled his housekeeper's ashes*." She paused and winced again. "What would you think?"

He tried not to smile. Elizabeth was nothing if not well-versed in slang. "I would think that the opposite was true," he admitted.

Elizabeth sat back. Having won a point in whatever competition they were engaged in, she slumped down in her chair as if she'd suddenly lost her steam.

"The problem is not without a solution," Harry said. "If the town has the wrong impression, then they've made a mistake based on appearances." He scratched his chin, deep in thought. "Perhaps I should make it known that your position here has changed. That you are assisting me in my research."

She shook her head. "A woman researcher? What manner of assistance could a woman possibly provide, besides the one they already imagine?"

Harry raked his hand through his hair. "If you know how wrongheaded they are, then why care what they think?"

"I don't care to be in either the minds or the mouths of the townspeople."

"That is certainly understandable. This is all quite frustrating, and since it is you who bears the brunt of the thing, it's wrong of me to question your feelings. But I can't help but wonder why this situation matters so very much. It's as if there are other considerations in play."

She brushed a strand of hair from her face.

"If appearances have led to a misunderstanding," he continued, "then the solution is to change appearances. You had originally intended to leave your parents' home when you had sufficient savings put aside. Landing here was an accident of sorts. We can find you a place of your own. This is a college town. There are a number of boarding houses that cater to students."

Elizabeth's mouth dropped open. After a moment, she stood and walked to her bedroom, closing the door behind her.

Nonplussed, Harry replayed their conversation in his mind, looking for clues. So terrible for her to be at the whim of rumor and innuendo—to care so much for the good opinion of misguided people. Terrible for the people of the town to be so quick to judgement.

Elizabeth walked out of her bedroom, still wearing her coat, her bag draped over her shoulder. "I will be leaving, then. I'm certain Mrs. Hartley will keep me until I can make other accommodations."

"Good God," Harry said, standing. His leg trembled beneath him. "Not today. It's Christmas!"

"I've made a mark against your reputation," she said, a touch of accusation in her voice. "I should not delay." She took a step toward the door.

"Stop!" he said, his voice raised, which caused them to look at each other in shock. "This is unreasonable."

"I wouldn't burden—"

"You're not a burden!"

She ignored him, hand on the doorknob.

"This is what you want? You don't want to be here?" he asked.

"This is for the best," she answered.

She's giving up her dream, he thought. *I mustn't let her.* He cleared his throat. "You will still assist me in the workshop?"

Her face crumpled. She opened the door. Wind and ice blew into the room.

"I must insist you continue your employment. I have become dependent on your help." He needed to staunch this unseen wound and give her something to hold onto.

"Men are such imbeciles," she said, her face flushed. "All they think about is their plans and concerns, as if nothing else matters. As if the heart means *nothing.*" She shook her head. "Yes, Professor. I'll work in your shop, until that, too, becomes a burden."

"I thought working in research was your dream?"

"It was!" she said, tears spilling from her eyes.

"Elizabeth." He stood, fingers to the table, propping him up. "I don't understand."

And then he did.

"You must give me a moment. There has been a terrible misunderstanding. I can make this right." He stepped away from the table, closed the front door, and led her to the table. "You must give me two minutes. That is all I ask. If, after two minutes, you still want to leave, I'll find you a carriage, Christmas Day or no."

She did not sit down. He moved toward his bedroom, walking backwards lest she make a run for the door. He ducked into the room, returning after only a few moments. "Please don't go," he said.

"It's for the best," she repeated.

"No, it's not. As I said, there's been a misunderstanding. I'm not speaking of the townspeople. I'm speaking of myself. Will you sit?"

"No," she said.

"All right, then," he said. "We'll stand here like statues and waste a perfectly good table. Tell me, aside from the condemnation of your family and everyone in town, is there another concern here? One involving me, perhaps?"

Her eyes went wide. "Are you *mocking* me?"

"No, no! But it's all quite funny, as you'll see in a moment. When I first hired—" he broke off, coughing into his fist. When he'd regained himself, he continued. "When I hired you, I had no idea that you desired to work in my field. No idea that you were so very accomplished. Once I realized the intensity of your enthusiasm, I couldn't allow anything to stand in your way, including my wishes."

"You didn't wish for me to work with you? You kept me on as a kindness?" Her tears threatened again.

"Good God, I'm making a mess of this." He fished into his pocket, withdrawing a small box. "I didn't want you to think that your employment was influenced by anything other than your excellence." He opened the box. "Work aside, I've fallen completely in love with you."

Silence.

He tried to hand her the ring, but she stood still, hands over her mouth. For one terrible moment, he thought she might abandon the cottage.

"Elizabeth?"

She stared at the ring, and then at him.

"I bought this ring in hopes that you might someday marry me—"

Elizabeth dropped her bag and launched herself at him, burying her face in his chest. Surprised, he nearly stumbled. She held him up, sobbing into his shirt. Smiling at last, he wrapped his arms around her, and there they stood for a very long time. When she finally recovered enough to look up, he kissed her.

CHAPTER SIXTEEN

Preparations/Three of Four/One Word

Ohio, 1921

Over the course of the following week, Harry made several trips into town. He visited Mrs. Hartley with a proposition. He visited Mr. Albanesi and placed an order, also borrowing the baker's phone to call Zanesville. Finally, he visited the church to talk with the pastor, who agreed to a mid-January date, providing that both Elizabeth and Harry went through a brief period of spiritual counseling.

"A church wedding is the first step in rehabilitating our image with the townspeople," Harry said. "A proper ceremony and regular attendance will erase any negative perceptions." Elizabeth had her doubts, but Harry promised her that most townspeople were like the Albanesi family. Hard workers with good hearts. "Besides," he added, "to know you is to love you."

"What about my family?" she asked.

"They are a separate issue."

Then, Harry explained his plan. Elizabeth would move in with Mrs. Hartley until the wedding. The widow would be instrumental in making their new situation known, since she possessed great skills in the art of rumor and gossip. "She has been frosty to me as of late," Elizabeth worried.

"I spoke to her at length, and she seems quite pleased to have such an important role in our rehabilitation," Harry said, smiling.

"I'll need a dress."

"Red velvet is nice," Harry said. When Elizabeth's expression fell, he smiled. "I ordered you a wedding dress from the shop in Zanesville," he explained. "We'll go there when the weather breaks. We'll make sure it's what you want."

"What about a reception?" she asked. "The bride's family is supposed to host a celebration." Once again, her expression fell.

"Mrs. Hartley offered to serve as hostess. She plans an afternoon luncheon and tea. And I ordered a fine cake from the bakers. Two layers with pillars between them."

"Oh, how wonderful!" Elizabeth said. Then she frowned again.

"You are full of hesitations," he complained.

"Must I move in with Mrs. Hartley?"

"It's perfectly normal for a housemaid to board at her place of employment, but it's not proper for a bride-to-be to live with her fiancé before the wedding. Our situation has changed, and we will follow custom."

Elizabeth sighed. "If it snows, I might not be able to come here. The cottage and our research will suffer."

"It's not ideal, I agree, but I will make do. I did so for some time before you arrived."

"I am feeling unneeded," she said, her lower lip extended in a pout.

He swept her into his arms. "You are needed."

"We shall make the best of it then," she vowed, gazing into his eyes. "If anyone asks, I'll tell them the bank's closed."

Harry burst out laughing. *No kissing or hugging.* Elizabeth's knowledge of slang was one more bit of wordplay that endeared her to him.

On the following day, the hired carriage arrived to escort Elizabeth to the widow's cottage. Harry accompanied her and helped the carriage driver unload her things. The widow Hartley scurried around giving directions in full bluster, which Harry took as a sign that she was quite happy to have a houseguest to direct, having had no one underfoot since her husband's demise.

Afterward, the carriage took Harry to town. He stopped to purchase lumber and other supplies, which were then delivered. One final task remained. The bed he'd purchased for Elizabeth's room was quite superior to the one he'd often avoided in his own room. The carriage driver helped Harry move the good bed to Harry's room and left with the other bed in tow, having a wholly unsatisfactory cot of his own at home that could now be replaced.

• • • • •

Elizabeth arrived for work the following morning. Harry shut Elizabeth's door, insisting that she stay out, reminiscent of his prohibition of the workshop when she first entered his employ. "It's a surprise," he said, and then ushered her into the workshop. "We are behind our schedule," he told her. "We have become slothful in our affection." His eyes shone when he said so, and she laughed to see how silly he'd become.

In the workshop, she returned to her copper winding. Meanwhile, Harry assembled his latest pieces on a sheet of butcher's paper on the long bench. He arranged the electromagnets according to his calculations, then ran current through them. His first step in studying the field was to measure the field strength with a magnetometer, a device that looked like a cross between a clock and a microscope. Elizabeth, being who she was, demanded a full demonstration of the device. Having made notes in her journal and made use of the device itself, she returned to her wiring with a smile on her face.

Next, Harry compared his calculations to the patterns on the paper using a sprinkling of iron filings, which situated themselves in field lines on the flat surface. Again, Elizabeth was called upon to do one of her fine journal drawings. Harry was amazed to see the accuracy of her depictions. He handed her his equations and asked her to add them beneath the drawing as a point of reference. "You will soon need a second journal," he said.

"We will need a shelf full of journals by the time our work is done," she answered.

Later, over dinner, she sat still, gazing at her meatloaf.

"Is something wrong with your food?" he asked. "Mine is quite excellent. You are a splendid cook."

"I was thinking about your machine," she said.

"What about it?"

"Your magnetic field. You situated it on paper, so that you could use the metal filings. Is that correct?"

"Yes."

"You told me you wished to create a magnetic field that would constitute a vortex from a four-dimensional perspective."

"Yes." Harry frowned. *What is she driving at?*

"It seems to me that constructing a predictable four-dimensional vortex would be more easily accomplished if you used the three dimensions available to you. Your equations are for a two-dimensional field you can place on your bench top. Easier to measure, I'm certain. I don't know how you'd be able to get the iron filings to float in the air, but—"

Harry stood up and strode to the workshop.

"Your meatloaf?" she asked.

He shut the door behind him, glancing back to offer her a hasty smile. *Good grief.* He tore a five-foot section of butcher's paper from the roll and spread it over the workbench, pressing it flat and writing in the upper left corner.

By the time she tapped at his elbow, he'd covered two-thirds of the sheet with his equations. He jumped at her touch. His hair splayed to the side, the result of absently raking his fingers over his scalp while he worked.

"It's late," she whispered.

He shook his head. "What time?"

"Nine," she said.

"How can that be?" he marveled. He glanced down at the butcher's paper—a mathematical roadmap for a journey to a destination no one living had visited before. He pointed at the figures. "This," he explained, pointing. "This is why I need you in my workshop. You are my compass. You keep me pointed in a practical direction."

"I needn't go to Mrs. Hartley's," she said. "I can stay. We are going to be wed."

"Yes, we are," he said. "But I will escort you home now. I am so sorry to have kept you." He stepped into the main room, which had been restored to its pristine ideal. "You made yourself busy in here."

"You needed time alone," Elizabeth said. She bundled herself into her new coat—still another of Harry's extravagances—and stepped into the night. "It's dark!" she said.

Harry paused to light a lamp. "No moon. No stars. The heavens don't seem to share my mood," he said. "I believe

I'm as happy as I've ever been. We're close to solving the problem, Elizabeth. I'm certain of it." He stopped in the middle of the road and tilted his head. "Thank you. Thank you for coming into my life."

She put her arms around him. "You are wearing the same threadbare coat that has kept you shivering all winter long. No more gifts. Not until you buy yourself a serviceable coat."

He leaned into her. "This is nice. We could stand here like this, right here in this spot, rather than continue down the road."

"You are an imbecile," she said.

"As you reminded me at Christmas. This time, I detect a hint of affection."

"Love," she said, correcting him. "Love everlasting."

·   ·   ·   ·

When he returned, he did not sleep. He'd originally intended to continue his work on Elizabeth's old bedroom. He had the shelving half-finished. He'd already displayed his own books. Gauss's *Disquisitiones Arithmeticae*. Ørsted's *Experimenta circa effectum conflictus electrici in acum magneticam*. Boole's *An Investigation of the Laws of Thought*.

Not all his titles were scientific. Hugo's *The Man Who Laughs*. Schenker's music theory texts, *Free Composition, Counterpoint,* and *Harmony*.

More books would arrive in the post, perhaps by the end of the month. Jane Austen's novels and books from each of three Brontë sisters. He could not wait to introduce her own personal library—his gift to Elizabeth on their wedding day.

Instead, he would translate the new equations into the magnetic field he'd imagined. He'd visualized what he needed, just as he'd once visualized an electric ignition system for the college president's Hudson. He used some of the bookshelf wood to construct the stand necessary for a three-dimensional field. Hopefully, the DC power from his batteries would be sufficient.

He staged the pieces and hooked up the speaker, the microphone, and other components. He worried that he'd wasted Elizabeth's time with the odd iron shapes, but after configuring the apparatus, he found they were useful indeed. His first effort yielded nothing more than static, of course. So much of what he was doing would require trial and error.

Sometime before morning, he stepped out of the cottage for some fresh air and was surprised to discover a blizzard in progress. The overcast skies had translated into a full-blown storm. The only light in the cottage was hidden in the workshop behind a closed door. The moon behind the clouds barely illuminated the field outside of his cottage. He could not make out the road. Wind swirled the flakes of snow. He could imagine a glistening tunnel—a vortex fashioned from shards of ice. For a moment, a sense of vertigo overtook him, and he grabbed for the frame of the cottage door for support. *When did I last sleep?* he wondered. He felt as if he might fall forward into the maelstrom, sucked into oblivion. He moved back inside, shaking from the cold and the trick of vision that had frightened him.

I need to eat, and I need to sleep. Elizabeth had left a muffin wrapped in paper in the cupboard. He shoved half of it in his mouth at once, his stomach growling. When had he left his meatloaf behind? Five o'clock? What time was it now? It wasn't good to push himself so hard.

He glanced at his bedroom door. Someday soon, she would join him there. He felt certain he would be able to sleep then, her hand on his back, her body curled into his. But not tonight.

Back in the workshop, he traced his equations. Two-thirds of the way through, he saw a simple error. *Sleepy fool!* He corrected the subsequent equations, which carried the echoes of miscalculation. When he finished, he adjusted the device and tried again.

"Hello?" He adjusted the variable capacitor systematically, forcing himself to rotate the plates in small, deliberate increments. "Hello?"

A sound. He stopped, noted the frequency setting, and tried again. "Hello?"

Nothing.

He pursed his lips. Producing positive results might validate his efforts. A negative result, however, meant one of two things—that he'd not solved the problem, or that the problem was unsolvable. Those two possibilities looked identical in the workshop.

He tried again. "Hello?"

Nothing.

He changed the frequency.

His leg had begun to tremble. Had he remembered to put the salve on the scar tissue? He couldn't recall. Either way, he couldn't stand anymore. He crossed the room, grabbed Elizabeth's stool, and placed it near the machine.

Wood was the right material for the three-dimensional staging because it was non-magnetic and electrically inert. But the device looked like something out of a child's drawing. If he'd solved the dilemma, he would craft a finer set of staged, angled wooden rings, vaguely spherical. He would varnish and polish them. The machine would look like a piece of modern art, like *Tatlin's Tower*. It would be beautiful.

"Hello?"

He turned to a higher frequency. The dial only turned so far. What would he try next? He needed to start over. To question every assumption. They had time. They would work on the machine together. She would not be sequestered at the widow's cottage forever.

He took another break, head aching. *I will check the weather, and then I'll finish up here. No more than another hour. Then I'll sleep. I'm doing myself no favors by staying awake.*

The sky outside hinted at morning, though the storm was in full force. The sight of the snow piling up disheartened him. Elizabeth would not be able to come in the morning. *She might try*—a thought that gave him a fright. He might have to walk to Mrs. Hartley's cottage to warn her against such foolishness.

Realizing how ridiculous that thought was, he shook his head.

Back inside, he went to the workshop, rubbing his eyes with sleep in mind.

I'll finish circumnavigating the tuner and then go to bed.

"Hello?" he asked.

Static. And then, a sound. He repeated his greeting but got no response. He nudged the tuner the smallest increment he could manage, and repeated, "Hello?"

A single word response, cutting through the static, clear as his speaker could manage.

Moribund.

CHAPTER SEVENTEEN

Conversations With a Dead Composer

Ohio, 1921

By mid-morning, drifts of snow covered the road, making it impassable. Harry resigned himself to working alone. His disappointment served as a catalyst, propelling him into the bedroom. He needed rest. One could not revisit complex calculations with a mind clouded by fatigue.

He awoke hours later, bathed in sweat, despite the cold. Restless dreams left him drained. The snow had ceased, but the temperature outside had plummeted. Harry tried to shake loose whatever nightmare had gripped him by starting a fire. His hands trembled and the fire sputtered. *My fingers are icicles,* he thought. When the kindling finally caught, he pulled the chair to the fire and sat down in front of it, rubbing his hands together.

Moribund. He'd heard the word, clear as the sun. But what did that mean? Had he discovered a new form of radio transmission that connected to faraway lands? Or was someone nearby having at him? He'd proven nothing. He needed Elizabeth to verify his steps.

Soon, the lure of the machine pulled him from his chair by the fire and returned him to the workshop. He forced himself to retrace his mathematical steps. He made minor adjustments to the machine and tried the microphone again.

Harry:"Hello?"

Voice:"Hello."

Harry: "To whom am I speaking?"

Voice:"To whom am I speaking?"

Harry stepped away from the bench. The conversation was not an accident of static. That much was certain. He tried hard to contain his excitement. He glanced at his hands. Warm now, but still trembling. He spoke into the microphone again.

Harry: "My name is Harry Browning. What is your name?"

Voice:[Silence]

Harry:"I would be grateful for a name."

Voice:"Alfred Stearns."

Harry wrote the name down on the butcher's paper, beneath the equations. He would ask questions. If the voice belonged to someone who'd died, the details might be verifiable. Those details would constitute proof of a sort.

Harry: "Where are you now?"

Alfred:"Where are you?"

Harry:"I am in New Concord, Ohio. Where are you?"

Alfred:"I [static] to say."

Harry:"Can you describe your location?"

Alfred:[Static] ". . . doesn't make sense."

Harry:"Alfred, do you recall the year of your birth?"

Alfred:"I was born in 1843."

Harry shook his head. The man might well be alive. That date of birth would put him in his late seventies. He longed to ask Alfred if he was dead, but such a question seemed both absurd and impertinent. Harry wished again that Elizabeth could act as his witness. She could record the conversation. She could suggest the right questions.

Harry:"What is your occupation?"

Alfred:"I am a composer."

Harry:"A composer of music?"

Alfred:[Silence]

Harry rubbed his eyes with his fists. Elizabeth was an accomplished piano player. She could talk to this disembodied voice. But she was not here. He would have to make do.

Harry:"Can you describe your present location?"

Alfred:"Why, I'm here. Right here."

Harry:"You are here in New Concord?"

Alfred:"I am here in this place."

Harry shivered and glanced around the room, half expecting to see the ghost of someone named Alfred hovering over his shoulder. The batteries that ran his lighting system had been taxed. The room had acquired a dim, amber glow. He gathered himself. This sort of nonsense would not do.

Harry:"Can you see me?"

Alfred:"I can tell you are [static]. But my vision is changed, as if I've rubbed my eyelids until all I can see is sparks and swirls."

Harry took a deep breath. He must ask the question. There was no alternative. He thought about the right phrasing and decided that a straightforward query was the most respectful.

Harry:"Are you living or dead, sir?"

Alfred:[Silence]

Harry:"If I've offended you—"

Alfred:"I must assume that I am dead. No other answer suffices."

Harry:"Can you tell me what you see?"

Alfred:"My senses [static] not operate."

Harry:"Yet you said that you were here. With me. How can you tell?"

Alfred:"I do not know. You are here, and we are communicating. I do not understand."

Harry:"You were born in 1843?"

Alfred:"Yes. In Berea, Ohio."

Harry:"When did you die? Do you know?"

Alfred:"1892."

Harry:"That's the year I was born.'

Alfred:"What year is it, then?"

Harry:"It's 1921."

Alfred:[Silence]

Harry:"Have you written music that I might be familiar with?"

Alfred:"I am writing still."

Harry:"I would like to play one of your compositions. How should I proceed?"

Alfred:[Silence]

Harry:"You are still writing? Still writing music?"

Alfred:"I can compose, but the notes are in my head. My mind."

Harry:"What compositions can I search for? Ones you wrote while still alive?"

Alfred:"[Static] dwarfed those works. Are you listening?"

Harry:"I'm here. The device I'm communicating with is imperfect."

Harry waited for an answer, but none seemed forthcoming. He tried conversing again, but Alfred Stearns would not—or could not—answer his questions. Harry longed to ask for details of the man's life. Something he could verify. Something that would serve as proof.

Stop. Proof would come in its own time. But what of Alfred? What must he yearn for? Harry thought he knew. *I must have disappointed the man horribly. I've been a dolt.*

Harry:"I am interested in the music you've written recently."

Alfred:[Silence]

Harry:"I cannot imagine that you are able to write it down."

Alfred:"No. I cannot."

Harry:"That must be a terrible frustration."

Alfred:[Silence]

Harry:"I am sorry, then. I wish I could help."

Alfred:"You could, of course."

Harry:"How can I help?"

Alfred:"I can dictate [static] you."

Harry:"I am musically illiterate. But my partner is an accomplished musician. I am certain she could write down your compositions, note for note, if that would give you some pleasure."

Alfred:"[Static] five parallel lines. Can you not manage that much?"

The voice, which had so far been flat, and yes, lifeless, had suddenly become animated. Excitement. Impatience? Harry asked for a moment's pause and rushed into his new, half-finished library. There, he grabbed a book on music theory—the future starting point for his eventual exploration of music. Returning to the workroom, he tore off a huge sheet of paper from the roll and spread it out next to his machine, on top of his equations. He flipped through the book, looking for an explanation of notation.

Alfred:"Are you there?"

Harry:"I'm here. I'm here. I am setting up a musical staff."

Alfred:"[Static] a clef."

Harry:"I don't know what that is."

Alfred:"Are you a child? Are you a dullard?'

Harry:"Please be patient. I've drawn the five staff lines."

Alfred: "[Static] Andante."

Harry followed the voice's directions, dividing the staff into measures, making notations he did not understand.

He was often unable to get the notes right the first time they were dictated, a frustration that sent Alfred into a rage. For Harry, who did not know a half note from a quarter note, the transcription was fraught with tension, though he was far too excited to take offense. What he was doing—taking dictation from beyond the mortal realm—was earth-shattering. Beyond anything he'd considered. Could he speak to those great minds long gone and obtain the thoughts they'd had since passing? Had the great writers of the last century continued writing stories in their minds? What wisdom might they impart?

As for Alfred Stearns, the composer gave him a few grudging bits of information interspersed with his flurried dictation. Born in Berea in a small house on old Bagley Road. His father made grindstones from sandstone taken from Rocky River, which flowed nearby. He was raised Methodist and took his schooling at Baldwin-Wallace College. His composition, *The Scarlet Tanager*, was popular in Europe. He died of tuberculosis. Each detail was delivered in a clipped, angry voice, as if answering Harry's questions diverted him from the task at hand.

Would Harry have been any different? By the man's account, he'd been dead for nearly three decades. Stearns was anxious to attend to his calling again.

One hour bent over the butcher's paper became two, then five. Harry's fingers cramped and his back ached. The worst of it was knowing that he couldn't be sure the notes he was writing were correct. He did not know music. But he did know math, and some of the changes did not make sense to him. One or two patterns repeated, but the notes seemed not to belong to each other. That was surely his error. Alfred Stearns could not see the paper, and Harry was reduced to repeating passages verbally, again and

again. When a mistake was made—and there were many—
Alfred flew into a snarling rage.

Harry:"I must take a break. I have to use the
bathroom."

Alfred:"We are not done! We've nearly reached the end
of the first movement!"

Harry:"How long is this piece?"

Alfred began cursing. Harry stepped away from the
bench, stunned. The man was not quite right. "You
understand, sir, that I will have to sleep eventually? I am
flesh and blood, sir." *And you are quite ungrateful.*

Alfred went silent again. Harry looked at the hastily
drawn notation, spread out over several feet of paper. He
would have to copy the piece. Perhaps someone in town
sold sheet music and could provide him with a useable
template. Either way, this endeavor would not be finished
in a single day.

Harry:"We've reached an end to our work today."

Alfred:[Silence]

Harry:"How do I reach you tomorrow? We can work on
this after I've slept."

Alfred:"I am here."

Harry:"So you said. Do I call for you?"

Alfred:[Silence]

Harry:"For that matter, how do I speak to others like
you? Are you alone there?"

Alfred:"We are *all* here."

This last gave Harry a chill, as if someone had run a
cold blade between his shoulders. He shivered. Sleeping
was questionable work for him as it was. The notion of
being surrounded by the dead while he slept made him
wonder if he could even close his eyes.

Harry:"There are others whom I wish to speak to. How
do I call to them?"

Alfred:"By name. If they wish to speak to you, they will."

Harry:"Can everyone hear me now?"

Alfred:[Silence]

Harry:"George. George Browning?"

Alfred:"No. We must finish the music."

Harry:"We will. But I want to speak to George Browning. My father."

Alfred:"He's not here now. He can't speak now."

Harry:"Alfred, I want you to listen to me. I've been very accommodating to you. I think it's time we establish some basic rules. This process must feature a give-and-take. So far, I give, and you take. Henceforth, there will be a trade-off. Is that clear?"

Alfred:[Silence]

Harry:"George Browning."

Alfred:"[Static] the music is finished. Not before."

CHAPTER EIGHTEEN

Contact/ A Small Lie/ Amelia

Ohio, 1921

The storm continued for three days, causing Harry great frustration. The date for his wedding had been chosen without regard to weather. Elizabeth's dress must be fitted. The pastor would have his say on the subject of matrimony. Preparations for the reception lay ahead. Accomplishing everything in time seemed impossible. But what weighed on him most was finishing the composition for Alfred Stearns.

Stearns had become unbearable. Between the composer's fits of anger and the storm outside, Harry found himself slipping into depression. Trying to sleep did nothing to alleviate the pressure inside his skull. Once in bed, Harry's sore eyes stayed open, gazing through the window at the blackness until morning painted the sky gray.

Each time Harry switched on his machine, Stearns was there waiting. On the third day, Harry tried incremental frequency changes, coupled with small changes to the field. With nothing to show for the effort, he returned to the original frequency and found that the *exact* setting was beyond the capability of his dial, which was how he encountered the second voice—a woman's voice.

Harry:"Hello? Can you hear me?"

Voice:"Yes. Yes! Hello?"

Harry:"My name is Harry Browning. What is your name?"

Voice:"Amelia Winters. I'm Amelia. Where are you?"

Harry:"I'm in New Concord, Ohio, madame. Where are you?"

For several long minutes, no answer was forthcoming. He was about to adjust the frequency again when he received an answer of sorts to his question. A keening wail, high-pitched, came unbroken, as if from a great distance.

Harry:"Miss Winters. Mrs. Winters? Amelia."

Amelia:"Where *are* you? I can feel you there, but I can't see you. I can't see anything at all. Your voice is not in my ears. It's in my head. Are you real?"

Harry:"I'm real."

Amelia:"I've prayed for you."

Harry clutched the microphone, his knuckles turning white. What must he say to this poor woman? He had so many questions, but her evident distress pushed them aside. He must try to offer some small comfort.

Harry:"Amelia. May I call you Amelia?"

Amelia:"Yes. Yes."

Harry:"I'm Harry Browning. I'm a scientist working in New Concord, Ohio. Do you know of the town?"

Amelia:"I [static] New Concord. Of course, I know of it. Am I in New Concord now? What is wrong with my eyes?"

Harry:"I am trying to find out what's happened to you, Amelia."

Amelia:"What's happened?"

Harry: "I need you to be calm, Amelia. Please try to describe your situation. Do any of your senses still work?"

Amelia:"I can hear you, but not with my ears. Your voice is like a shadow."

Harry dared not touch the dial, lest he lose this contact. He wanted to ask her about her life—and yes, her death.

He wondered if she even realized she'd passed through the veil. Was that possible? What would the revelation of her death do to her?

Harry:"Amelia. I'm here. Focus on my voice."

Amelia: "I'm alone."

Harry:"You are not alone. I'm here with you."

The keening returned. Then, more static.

The machine was not at all what he'd imagined. What had he expected? A tearful reunion with those who'd been taken from him, of course. That was the real reason he'd undertaken the quest. But this? This gave him a sinking feeling that pulled him deep into his trench of depression. His mine shaft. His vortex. He closed his eyes and rubbed his forehead.

Alfred:"What are you doing? What have you done with my music?"

Harry:"Alfred? Where is Amelia?"

Alfred:"We have to finish the music, you worthless mutton monger. You bracket-faced fumbler."

Harry:"Alfred, the music is nearly transcribed. I have been a tireless servant in this regard. You will change your tone with me, sir."

Alfred:"Finish. We must finish."

Harry:"I am speaking to Amelia. Let me speak to her."

Alfred:"Finish."

Harry:"Amelia? Can you hear me?"

Alfred: "Finish."

Harry switched off the machine. The composer had waited nearly thirty years to ply his trade. Now, he would wait a little more. Harry strode from the workshop, shutting off the lights as he went.

He paused by the dining table. Outside, the sun was making a modest appearance. The wind had settled. Harry realized he had absolutely no idea what time of day it was.

His watch had stopped dead for lack of winding. He stepped out into the frigid air and made his best guess based on the position of the sun. Nearly noon, he decided. He needed no further enticement. He donned dry socks, his coat, and a scarf. Giving the main room a final glance, he headed into the snow.

·   ·   ·   ·   ·

He passed Mrs. Hartley's cottage on his way to town. If he stopped, he would go no further. He would not be able to leave Elizabeth's side. Instead, he walked to the church to speak with the pastor. He found him in the church—a stroke of luck, for if he'd been elsewhere, Harry would not have known where to look. He did not know the man's address. He could hardly go door-to-door, banging on shutters.

Pastor Frederick was a tall, thin sort of man with a high forehead and a crop of thick, wavy hair that surrounded the back of his head like a great white manicured shrub. He wore ill-fitting glasses, such that he constantly returned them to the bridge of his nose with his index finger. His lips were thin, and his smile kindly. He greeted Harry warmly and remarked, "You and your bride-to-be missed our session."

"The storm had other ideas in mind," Harry said. "But I take these sessions seriously and hoped to reschedule for the day after tomorrow."

"Yes," Pastor Frederick said, pushing at his glasses. "But we were already scheduled for that day as well."

"Time being of the essence, I'd hoped we could double our efforts then, the wedding day being already selected."

"You are in a great hurry."

Harry could detect no malice in the statement. "Our living situation is unique," he explained. "I am loathe to be separated from her. Being alone—"

"Ahhh," the pastor said, nodding with understanding. "You miss both a companion and a housekeeper."

Harry was silent.

"Well, we'll do our best, then. We will be seeing you both on a regular basis after the wedding, will we not?"

"As promised," Harry said. He stood and turned to leave but then remembered his other reason for visiting. "Pastor Frederick. You know nearly every person in New Concord."

"Very nearly," he agreed.

"And I suppose you knew many who've passed on?"

"Yes," he said, his voice mournful. "The Great Flu has taken far too many as of late."

"Did you ever meet Alfred Stearns, the composer?"

The pastor's head bobbed, a surprised look on his face. "Why, yes. I believe we even have the sheet music for one of his pieces. Excellent music. Our organist, Mrs. Torrance, used to play the piece after the recessional. Something for people to exit to."

"Did you ever know the man? I believe he died sometime in the nineties."

The pastor nodded. "Oh, yes. He was much beloved here. Lived out the end of his life in New Concord. A finer man, you could not hope to meet. I was just a boy then. He treated me very well, as I recall."

"Fascinating," Harry said. "Now, let me ask you about a second name."

After completing his errands, he headed for Mrs. Hartley's, a pack of music staff paper under his arm. As he approached the gate, Elizabeth burst from the front door without a coat, her arms open to him. Harry cut their embrace short, herding her back inside, out of the cold. "You'll catch your death."

"And you!" she cried. "Your hands are blue! What were you thinking?"

"I was thinking that I needed to see my Elizabeth."

Mrs. Hartley stood near her oven, clucking. "We saw you pass by on your way to town without stopping. Our dear girl nearly went into paroxysms."

"Oh, no, it wasn't so bad as that," Elizabeth said, blushing.

"No matter," Harry said. "I've missed you terribly."

Mrs. Hartley sat them both at the table and scurried around her kitchen, putting on the tea-kettle and plating a handful of cookies that she'd not yet eaten. Harry sat shivering, his eyes on the window. The sun would be going down soon.

"I can't stay long."

Elizabeth started to speak but Mrs. Hartley was quicker. "We'll get some hot tea inside you for the trip home," she promised.

Elizabeth grabbed his hands, rubbing them gently with her own. "Your fingers are icicles," she said.

"I'm fine," he said. "Now."

She looked away, stammering. "You worked without me, I suppose?"

Harry nodded, eager to tell her the news.

She bit her lip. "I very much hope to be there with you when your—" She glanced at Mrs. Hartley. "When your experiments bear fruit."

Mrs. Hartley stopped, a dishrag in her hands.

"Elizabeth has been assisting me with my research," Harry explained.

"That's very nice," Mrs. Hartley said.

"She has a degree from Muskingum," he added. "She's quite accomplished."

"When I was young," Mrs. Hartley said, "young girls learned to cook and sew and keep house." She folded the dishrag and put it on the sink. "Girls today have different chances, and I say, congratulations to them!"

Elizabeth grinned.

"At any rate," Harry said, "I've missed Elizabeth's help in the workshop. I can't quite do without her."

"I will be home soon," she promised. "And we will solve this particular problem." She leaned forward. "I miss our time working together."

Harry gave her a single, solemn nod.

"What are you working on?" Mrs. Hartley asked.

"A new kind of telephone." Elizabeth's smile was radiant. "We're going to change the world."

Harry smiled. "We certainly will."

• • • •

Returning to the cottage plunged him back into his previous depression. Alfred was waiting for him, of course, demanding he work on the composition. More meaningless notes, jumbled on butcher paper. *I will transfer this to the sheet music later,* he thought. But first, he needed to be certain. The previous four measures seemed more random, more disordered than before.

Harry:"I should like to be certain I have written these notes correctly." Alfred:"You are maddening."

Harry:"I am helping to bring your music to the world. I am surprised at your lack of appreciation. I have offered repeatedly to have you dictate your work to my assistant once the weather releases its grip."

Alfred:"Your telegraph is clever. I'll grant you that much."

Harry:"What will we do with the finished work? Have you decided?"

Alfred:"Until we finish, it is not a finished work."

•   •   •   •   •

"It's done," Harry announced. The stack of music sheets, carefully transcribed from his notes on butcher paper, sat on the corner of the long bench next to his machine. He'd copied the piece, note for note.

Alfred Stearns did not speak for a long time. When he did, his voice was quiet.

Alfred: "What will become of my music?"

Harry:"What would you have me do?"

Alfred:[Static.]

Harry:"There are a number of choices. Eventually, I'll be able to demonstrate the machine, and your music could be the first thunderclap in a scientific storm. You will be quite famous. I don't know if acclaim matters to you, Alfred. I think that perhaps only the music matters. But music is meant to be heard. Is that what you wish? For your music to be heard?"

Alfred:"What about now? What will you do with it *now?*"

Harry:"I have a piano. If I knew how to play, I'd play it for you. I could set the machine by the piano." [Pause] "Here's an idea—would you like to hear it played?"

Alfred:"Is such a thing possible?"

Harry:"My assistant will be here next week. My wife. Actually, she's going to be my wife. We're to be married on Wednesday."

Alfred:"If she played the piece for me, I would be grateful. But it must be a surprise."

Harry:"You shall hear your music again soon. By the way, have you named the piece?"

Alfred:"*Revanche*. Do you know the meaning?

Harry:"It has something to do with the Franco-Prussian War, does it not?"

Alfred:"Yes, France's desire for the return of Alsace–Lorraine. The return of things lost."

Harry:"By the way, the people in New Concord still remember you. You were well regarded in your later years. The church still plays a piece of your music at the end of services."

Alfred:"And I remember them, too."

Harry:"Are you tired, Alfred? Do you get tired?"

Alfred:[Silence]

Harry:"Alfred, I'm going to try to speak to other people. You seem to know how to get my attention when you wish to be heard. I encourage you to continue."

Alfred did not answer. Harry cleared his throat and asked, "Is Amelia there? Amelia Winter?" He wanted to call for his father instead. But he had news for Amelia, and he did not wish to wait. He repeated her name several times, but no one answered.

He tried small adjustments to the frequency. Just as he was about to abandon the effort, he made contact.

Harry:"Hello Amelia."

Amelia:"You went away!"

Harry:"Yes, but I came back. And I came back with news."

Amelia:[Silent]

Harry:"Tell me, Amelia. What do you remember of your daughter?"

Amelia:"Daughter?"

Harry:"Your daughter Louise."

Amelia:"Louise."

Harry: "Yes. Do you recall the accident, Amelia? You were walking on the old National Road. It was near dusk. A cart came speeding by—"

Amelia:"I remember. My poor Louise. [Static] her."

Harry:"Do you remember the cart striking you, Amelia?"

Amelia:"No. The cart struck Louise."

Harry:"The cart struck you both. Do you remember?"

Amelia:"My poor Louise!"

Harry:"Amelia? That's my news. Louise is fine. She survived. She's an old woman now, living in New Concord. She has two children and three grandchildren. You're a great-grandmother, Amelia."

Amelia:"Louise [Static] just a little girl.

Harry:"It was a long time ago, Amelia. Does it seem like a long time to you? Your daughter is grown."

Amelia:"My daughter is *dead*."

Harry:"No, no. Amelia, listen to me. Take heart. Your daughter is alive and well. She's happy. Very happy."

Amelia:[Silence]

Harry:"I'd like to help you remember."

Amelia:"I don't remember. I can't remember anything. I could remember once."

Harry:"I'd like to help you."

Amelia:[Silence]

·   ·   ·   ·   ·

Harry paused in his work to think about the conversation with Amelia Winters. A disturbing notion had occurred to him, one born of a childhood amongst the Presbyterians.

Harry's own religious notions were not fully formed. He preferred data to dogma, and in matters of heaven and hell, data was in short supply. His belief in God came from his observation of the details in nature. Something designed, down to a cellular level, must have a designer. Like the cosmological arguments of Aquinas, the idea of intelligent design did not mesh easily with tales of fire and brimstone.

Now, because of his machine, he must consider a question. To whom or what was he speaking when he turned on his machine? How close was the burnt chlorine smell of ozone to the stench of sulphur?

His uneasy suspicion could be tested, of course. He would ask to speak to Mr. Brympton, the finest man he'd ever known.

Returning to the lab, he began calling for his mentor, and just before dusk, he found him. Harry changed his working hypothesis once Brympton began to cry.

CHAPTER NINETEEN

The Wedding/ The Reception/ The Confession

Ohio, 1921

The day of the wedding arrived, both too soon and too late for Harry's satisfaction. The hurried trip to Zanesville for the dress, the matter of invitations, and the purchase of supplies for the reception were all accomplished at the very last moment. Harry longed for Elizabeth's return to the cottage, but found himself wishing for an extra few days' time as well. He wanted her wedding to be everything that she hoped for, not a patched together, rag doll sort of celebration.

He'd chosen a Wednesday for the ceremony, with a nod to the old folk rhyme:

Marry on Monday for health,
Tuesday for wealth,
Wednesday the best day of all...

Mrs. Hartley, who'd become very much the doting aunt, was instrumental in pulling together the final preparations. Without her assistance, the matter would have collapsed on itself like a dying star.

Harry thought it important to extend an invitation to the entire congregation, and then worried no one would attend. Mrs. Hartley assured him that would not be the case.

Harry had other errands that demanded his attention. He slept little, hurrying to finish Elizabeth's library. Some of the books he'd ordered arrived on time. The bulk, however, were presumably en route, floating somewhere in the postal system. Without them, the shelves looked bare. Harry consoled himself with the thought that there were enough books to give a general impression of what the room would be some day in the future.

He also paid a visit to Elizabeth's parents. Custom dictated that the bride's parents host the reception. Harry patiently explained why Mrs. Hartley would serve in that capacity, and the Roses did not object. "We certainly don't have the resources for this foolishness," Mrs. Rose stated. Harry explained the other peculiarity of the wedding plan and encountered some resistance. Rutherford argued in favor of walking down the aisle with his daughter, but his wife silenced him with a single admonition. "You're too fat to give her away."

The man's weight had nothing to do with the decision. Elizabeth would give herself away. She was not her father's property, nor was she Harry's. Marriage was her choice. The congregation might object, but Harry did not think so. They knew Rutherford Rose. No further explanation need be offered.

The counseling sessions with Pastor Frederick were awkward, fumbling exercises. Elizabeth was outspoken enough to put the wedding in jeopardy. She sat, hands folded in her lap, for the discussion about God's sovereignty over the gift of marriage. Likewise, was she silent when the pastor discussed the choice between fidelity in marriage and chastity in singleness. The session took a different turn when he ventured God's opinion of marital roles, quoting Corinthians 11:3: "The head of every man is Christ; and the head of the woman is the man." As

Harry later explained to Mrs. Hartley, "Elizabeth . . . disagreed."

Harry, adept at facilitating the appearance of agreement where none existed, was able to steer the discussion with tales of how he mentored Elizabeth in the lab, how cooperative she was, and in the end, the pastor was either satisfied or simply too exhausted to continue, giving his blessing to the union.

The night before the wedding, Harry was completely unable to sleep. He worried that his appearance might suffer—he'd lost weight in the past few weeks, in no small part because of his research. But fatigue was not enough to curb the excitement he felt. Elizabeth would be coming home. Home. The cottage would sing again. They would address the new problem together. His one conversation with Mr. Brympton left him deeply disturbed. He needed to discuss the matter with Elizabeth. Together, they would find a solution.

He arrived at the church hours early and found only the pastor. The Christmas roses Harry had gathered sat limp in two vases near the altar. He'd imagined them to be more inspiring, but the church was large, and the vases were small. Pastor Frederick put a hand on his shoulder and told him not to worry. "Everything will be just as it should be."

"I wonder if anyone will attend," Harry said, rubbing his sweaty palms together.

"You've invited God to your wedding," the pastor said. "He will be there."

The first person to arrive at the church was an effervescent Mrs. Hartley, who wore a dress she'd recently let out, along with a wide-brimmed hat festooned with yarn flowers. Harry gave her a hug and a kiss on the cheek. Greetings over, the widow set about attending to details. The pastor, who seemed somewhat in awe of the widow, hurried to help her. Mrs. Torrance had not yet arrived, but the pastor assured the widow that the organist would not be late.

Harry, who could barely stand the slow tick of the clock, stepped outside to walk the grounds behind the church. No wind—a blessing—but the cold might keep guests away. He paced through the trees, winding in a giant figure eight. At the far side of the path he was cutting, he spotted the arrival of a carriage. *Thank goodness!* he thought. He put his head down and concentrated on the infinity sign he'd dug in the snow. It took him half a minute to walk the full loop. If he made a hundred such circuits, he could go inside and see what sort of crowd had come to celebrate.

Around the seventieth turn, he realized he'd lost count. When his feet were nearly frozen, he returned to the church.

Carriages were parked everywhere. A few automobiles as well. The church was nearly full. Mrs. Hartley stood waiting for him, with what might have been tears glistening in her eyes. "They are here, just as I said they would be," she gushed. "For you, Professor, and for your dear girl."

Harry stood, open-mouthed. The people of the town turned to smile. The pastor waited near the altar.

Mrs. Hartley whispered, "She's in the façade tower," pointing to the side room near the entrance. "We're waiting for you."

"How long have I been gone?" he asked.

"You were nervous." Mrs. Hartley urged him forward. Harry took a deep breath and walked up the aisle, trying to return the smiles of the good people of New Concord.

The pastor took his place at the altar, motioned for silence, and offered an opening prayer.

After the singing of a hymn, the organ began the familiar strains of Felix Mendelssohn's wedding march. Harry, whose thoughts were hopelessly scattered, reminded himself that the music was originally written for a performance of Shakespeare's *A Midsummer Night's Dream*. Not his favorite of the plays. He tended to appreciate the lesser tragedies, like *Troilus and Cressida*, but—

Then he saw his bride.

Elizabeth walked alone, clutching a huge bouquet of flowers—surely the handiwork of Mrs. Hartley! She wore a cloche hat, fitted with a veil. Her dress was slim-waisted with ornate beading across the front. As she passed, people whispered and stared, perhaps because she walked alone, or perhaps because she was the distilled vision of everything smart and kind and beautiful in the world.

For his part, Harry had purchased a tie. His old suit jacket still fit, though it hung loose on his frame.

The pastor spoke, but with blood pounding in his ears, Harry couldn't make out a word. He tried to focus but could not. He heard the phrase, "to assist each other in all good things," and he smiled. Glancing to the side, he saw her in profile, head bowed and eyes closed.

The pastor asked the congregation for objections to the marriage. There being none, the pastor asked for declarations of consent from both Harry and Elizabeth. Then, the pastor paused for a moment. Harry realized that he was stumbling over the portion of the ceremony when the bride would be given away. The pastor had explained that there must be a "transfer of authority," and Harry held firm in refusing this one aspect. Otherwise, they would go to a justice of the peace and be done with it. But

Pastor Frederick was not a strict conformist, and Harry was not an iconoclast, so an agreement was struck between them, citing the bulk and health of Rutherford Rose. Now, his fumbling over, the pastor offered a prayer, a brief passage from the Bible, and finally, an exchange of vows. After one final prayer, he pronounced them husband and wife. Harry swept Elizabeth into his arms and kissed her.

"My friends," the pastor said to the congregation, "It gives me great pleasure to present to you, Mr. and Mrs. Browning of New Concord, Ohio."

∙　　∙　　∙　　∙

"Not everyone will attend the reception," Mrs. Hartley had told him.

She was very nearly wrong.

Those who could not squeeze into the cottage stood on the lawn. Mrs. Hartley raced from group to group, distributing baked goods, her overpreparation having been severely tested. Harry saw smiles everywhere. The sun made an appearance, a most welcome midday warming. Harry shook hands with more people than in his previous years in town combined. Names were put to faces, and though he vowed that he must remember them—he had learned Latin and Greek, after all—he found himself quickly overwhelmed.

The Roses arrived by carriage, as he'd previously arranged. The reception being an extension of the church ceremony, Mrs. Hartley's spirits stayed in the cupboard, but Rutherford Rose had his own resources. He wobbled while exiting the carriage, and nearly fell on his face on the lawn. Mrs. Rose, who'd managed a new dress for the event (again, courtesy of Harry Browning), looked dour, her mouth set in a hard line. They stood at the far end of the yard, at the fringe of the crowd, and Harry realized he would have to bring Elizabeth to them.

He found her inside the cottage, standing still as a statue while several women examined her dress. "So beautiful, my dear," one said. "The bead-work is exquisite."

"Elizabeth?"

"Yes, Professor?"

He led her to the yard. "Are you going to call me Harry, now that we're married?" he asked.

"Perhaps not," she said. "Perhaps it will be our private joke, even if only one of us finds it amusing." She stopped. Ahead, the Roses stood, Rutherford with his hand on the fence rail and Constance with her gnarled hands folded in front of her. "Who invited them?" she asked.

"I did."

"Why would you do that?" she whispered.

"For the same reason you send them money each week. Because they are your parents, and you are their daughter. It's time that we attempt a reconciliation, which must always begin with forgiveness."

Elizabeth nodded, and then glanced up. "You will do all of the cleaning this week," she said. She stepped forward to greet the Roses. Rutherford said something about how beautiful Elizabeth looked. Her mother's silence was mitigated by the amazing Mrs. Hartley carrying a plate with two pieces of Albanesi's wedding cake. Rutherford made quick work of one piece, and then stripped the icing from half of the other.

"I'm very glad you came," Elizabeth said. Her stone-faced mother didn't answer. When Harry suggested that they circulate and try to say hello to everyone, Constance stepped forward and grabbed Elizabeth by the forearm.

Her expression was stern, but she held her chin up and her shoulders back, something she seldom did. "You have *everything* I ever wanted," she said. Elizabeth froze. "And well you should. You are my daughter."

Elizabeth gave her mother a careful hug, as if the woman were made of glass, and then turned to go. Harry caught a glimpse of his bride's face. Tears shimmered in her eyes, but she wore a smile.

· · · · ·

The guests in the yard stood in groups, chatting and shivering, smiles on their faces. Harry helped Mrs. Hartley deliver food and drinks. Occasionally, from the corner of his eye, he'd spot a disapproving glare. A few conversations stopped at his approach, and he understood that not everyone approved.

But without exception, they enjoyed Mr. Albanesi's cake.

By late afternoon, the sky clouded over, dropping the temperature again. People said their final, happy goodbyes and rushed off into the gathering dusk. A few still bore frowns, of course. The world would always have its share of judgement and anger. Harry had always listened to the quieter voices, where love and reason resided.

Mrs. Hartley sat exhausted at her table. Having made the trip to her cottage, many townspeople left with jars of preserves and aged cheeses. She'd sold every egg and every pint of cream. "I'm quite wealthy now," she confided.

"I will never be able to thank you enough," Harry said.

"You're going, of course. You have business to attend to."

"I thought we'd stay and help you clean up."

Mrs. Hartley's laughed. "Pish. Be off with you."

Outside, Harry lifted Elizabeth up into the carriage and climbed in beside her. He'd remembered blankets this time, and they were both quite comfortable. Elizabeth put her head on his shoulder as they rode. The sky was too overcast for stars, so he was pleased they would arrive at the cottage before dark.

Her small voice interrupted his thoughts. "There is something I must discuss with you, husband."

He smiled.

"You will be angry with me, but it can't be helped. While I was at Muskingum, I was fond of a boy. He died in the war. If he'd come back, we might have married. His name was Walter Raymond."

Harry frowned. "What are you telling me?"

She clutched his arm tighter. "I was young, and we were close."

"Did you not save yourself for marriage?" His surprise gave way to his usual good nature. "It's all right. I won't be angry."

"I did save myself. In a manner of speaking. But there was a great deal of kissing and—"

Harry laughed. The carriage driver sat hunched in front of them, so Harry was discreet. "Thank goodness," he said. "I have no experience of any sort to bring to our union. One of us has a general idea of how to proceed."

At first, she was quiet. Then, she began to shudder. After a moment, he realized she was stifling her laughter. She whispered into his ear. "I'd imagined that you'd consulted a book."

He nodded in agreement. "I did, of course."

•　　•　　•　　•　　•

Much later, nestled in bed, spent, Harry lay on his back, struggling to stay awake and savor her warmth, her touch.

Outside, a front coming from the north blew the clouds away, leaving a cold, crystalline sky without a moon. Elizabeth had fallen asleep on his chest. He could feel her breath on his skin. He gazed through the window at the stars, thanking each one until he slipped into the deepest sleep he'd had in years.

•   •   •   •   •

In the morning, Harry sat her at the kitchen table and said, "I am going to cook you breakfast. Mrs. Hartley sent us with her last two eggs and a wedge of her cheese. You may not know this, but I am an expert at omelets."

"I am aware you speak French, so I am not surprised."

"Not a French omelet. An American omelet. Crispier, with heartier fillings. In this case, some of Mrs. Hartley's cheddar and some chopped sausage. How does that sound?"

"It sounds like you're trying to fatten me up," Elizabeth laughed. "I am unable to resist, since I am ravenous."

"Ravishing," he corrected. He beat the eggs, adding a touch of cream and a pinch of salt. The skillet already held diced sausage and the top of a green onion. He poured the eggs into the skillet and covered them with shreds of Mrs. Hartley's cheese. Then, he folded the mixture over and set it aside while he toasted bread. Giving each of them half, he set the food on the table.

"I have another surprise for you."

"Besides breakfast?"

"Yes," Harry said. "Look in your room."

Elizabeth shoveled a huge bite of omelet into her mouth and walked to the door where she stood for a moment, transfixed. "Oh, Harry!" she said, her voice muffled by egg and sausage. "Harry!"

The room had permanent shelves on three sides. The fourth side, with the window facing the trees behind the cottage, had a rolltop desk. "The desk didn't arrive until the day before yesterday," he said. "As it is, the shelves are scandalously bare. More books are on the way, but I believe that the postal service delivers parcels by tortoise-back."

By then, Elizabeth had swallowed her mouthful. She grabbed him by the shirt and pulled him close. "Harry."

"You will have to decorate. This is your room." He looked down, licking his lips. "Now, I have a confession to make."

"What is it?" she asked, smiling. She searched his face and stepped back, saying, "You finished the machine. It works."

He sighed. "Your suggestion for altering my equations—"

She rushed to the workshop and threw the door open. The machine sat on the long bench. The hasty wooden framework had been replaced by a series of ascending rings, some tilted. Electromagnets were fixed to the rings in odd positions. Because the taller rings were smaller, the contraption looked like a ziggurat. The tuner had been modified. The semicircular metal plates of the variable capacitor were the same, but the rotor now featured a dial mechanism that looked as if it had been fashioned by clock parts. "I needed a more precise control of the frequency," he explained.

"This works?" she asked. She reached out and touched the wooden frame. "This works!" Her high-pitched voice betrayed her excitement. "Harry!"

"I meant to tell you last week, but you'd have been so disappointed—"

"Who have you talked to?" she demanded.

"Four people, so far." Harry's expression fell. "The results have been somewhat disturbing. I will tell you everything, so that you can make notes in the journal." Then his face brightened. "But one of the men I spoke to was a composer—*is* a composer. Pastor Frederick knew him. I verified his story as much as I could. He died in 1892, the year I was born."

"Oh," she said, running a finger over the speaker. "This is extraordinary!"

Harry nodded. "I left out the best part. The composer, Alfred Stearns, blessed us with a new composition. I transcribed the piece, dictated from the grave, so to speak."

"Music?"

Harry grinned. "I knew you'd be excited. I have it here." He crossed the room to the parts shelf and grabbed a stack of papers. "Later, we'll set the machine by the piano, so you can play his composition for him. I've told him what an accomplished pianist you are." He held out the papers, and Elizabeth took them.

She glanced down at the first page, smiling. Then, the corners of her smile turned down, and her brow furrowed. Her mouth flew open. She glanced at Harry—wide-eyed—and then back at the page. Her head lurched back as if she were gagging. She met Harry's gaze again as tears of blood began to form in the corners of her eyes. She swiped a hand across the bridge of her nose, splattering crimson droplets across the front of her nightshirt. She whispered Harry's name and staggered as blood began to run from her eyes in rivulets.

CHAPTER TWENTY

The Devil's Chord/A Hypothesis

Ohio, 1921

Doctor Kemp closed the bedroom door behind him as he left the room, pulling off his mask. He presented himself to Harry with an expression of sorrow on his face. His salt-and-pepper goatee hooked to the side like the bottom stroke of a cursive J. His eyes, cracked and old, told a tale of woe that Harry could scarcely bear to hear. "You must brace yourself, sir. I'm afraid that the Great Flu has visited your household."

Harry paused his fears long enough to tilt his head and frown. "That makes no sense," he said at last. "On your last trip here, you said that a fever and chills were no indication of the flu. Today, she has none of the usual symptoms, and yet you saddle her with what might be a death sentence. How do you explain the blood, sir?"

Doctor Kemp shrugged helplessly. "She has a hyphema. Blood cells accumulate within the anterior chamber of the eye. Elizabeth's case is the worst I've seen, by far."

"What does that have to do with the flu?"

Again, the doctor shrugged. "The usual cause is some sort of physical trauma to the eye. But there are other causes, some of them quite mysterious. I suspect that the flu has elevated internal pressures behind the eye."

"What remedies do you have?"

He shook his head. "There is a vaccine available that directly addresses *bacterium Haemophilus,* though it does not prevent the flu. I'm told it lessens the death rate, but I am uncertain of the effect on patients who already have the disease, and I would not risk an injection. Nor would I know how to obtain the vaccine on such short notice."

"If you know where the vaccine is stored, I will go there myself."

"As I said, I don't know the effects on a patient already suffering. I would not venture to take the chance."

Harry glanced to the side. There, at the kitchen table, lay the tiny pile of sheet music. "I don't think it's the flu."

"That is my best diagnosis at this time," Dr. Kemp said. "I'm going to prescribe a regimen of aspirin, castor oil, and quinine. If she does not respond, we will try strychnine. As before, keep her hydrated. If you have pen and paper, I will write down a full list of instructions for you."

Harry brought paper and pen to the kitchen table. While the doctor bent over his work, writing so slowly that he might have been carving instructions on a clay tablet, Harry stood at the sink. The knot in his stomach had doubled on itself. "Doctor, I must ask a favor."

"Hmmm?" The doctor remained fixed on his instructions.

"Your trip home will pass by the widow Hartley's cottage. Will you please tell her what's happened, and ask if she will come? I have things I must do, and I cannot leave my wife alone."

"Of course," Doctor Kemp said. He paused in his work. "I enjoyed the reception there," he added. "I was surprised at the general good feeling, given the radical departure from tradition. A most unusual wedding. I refer to the absence of her father from the ceremony."

"Was it so great a departure?"

"I believe so," the doctor answered. "Young people have their own ideas. I'll say that much."

"Were people upset?"

"Not upset, per se. Perhaps they were surprised. A few probably worried over it."

"I wonder," Harry said, "how many of them will ascribe Elizabeth's illness to heavenly retribution." The thought was unkind, and he silently reprimanded himself.

At this, the doctor looked up from his work. "People are quite attached to their beliefs. They interpret the most random of occurrences through the temple of those beliefs." He paused. "Doctors, too." He fumbled briefly with his goatee and returned to the pen and paper. "I assume you have no quinine in the house?"

"None," Harry said.

"I will find a way to send some with the widow Hartley."

•　　•　　•　　•　　•

Once the doctor was gone, Harry glanced in at Elizabeth. She slept, and he was careful not to wake her. Part of him felt a wave of relief. Her soft brown eyes had turned black, and the sclera was shot through with red and black veins. If she recovered, her vision might not. He immediately set about solving that problem in his mind. Handrails throughout the cottage. He would build a back porch with a door from the bedroom and a chair in place so she could enjoy the outdoors without struggling to find her place. The library was a cruel joke now, of course. How could she—"

He was being absurd. He had no idea what was coming and no business anticipating. He would have to wait, like other mortals. He scowled. Of what use was his intellect if the result was pain inflicted on the one person he loved most? He'd done this to her. Alfred Stearns had fashioned a bomb, and Harry had dropped it in her lap.

He went into the workshop and closed the door. When he fired up the machine, Alfred was waiting for him.

Alfred:"Did your new wife enjoy my music?"

Harry:"What did you do?"

Alfred:"What did *we* do, you useless foozler. You played your part."

Harry:"Why didn't the music hurt me? Why did it only hurt my wife? Did you target her somehow?"

Alfred:"You can't read music, you illiterate dolt."

Harry:"How do I undo the damage?"

Alfred:"You can't."

Harry:"What did you do? *How do you undo it?*"

Alfred:[Laughter]

•   •   •   •   •

Mrs. Hartley sat with Elizabeth, changing the washcloth over her eyes, administering quinine and castor oil according to the doctor's notes, while Harry went into town. Class was not in session, but the caretaker let Harry into the Muskingum library, where he began his analysis of Alfred's sheet music. He found nothing of note in the music texts, so he expanded his search.

A small room at the rear of the library housed a single floor-to-ceiling bookshelf. Here, the oldest, most valuable, or most dangerous books were kept, including a pristine copy of Audubon's *Birds of America*, an early edition of Cotton Mather's *On Witchcraft*, and *De Institutione Musica* by Boethius. Harry's search was uncharacteristically haphazard, and nearly a full day's study gave him only three clues, but they coincided with his suspicion. The music composed by Alfred Stearns was a weapon.

The opening two-note chord was a tritone—a C and an F#—not found together in any major or minor scale. In the 17th century, the Catholic Church had outlawed the harmonically dissonant sound, calling it the "Devil's Chord."

Harry had already noted the mathematical irregularities of the composition. Because medieval liturgy was performed *una voce*—in unison—discordant sounds were regarded as the machinations of demons, promoting *effectus musicae*—infectious music.

The most telling clue involved an obscure Dutch painter named Hieronymus Bosch, who'd died in the early 1500s. Little was known of Bosch past his association with a local religious group and his influence on subsequent artists, including Peter Breughel the Elder. Bosch's most famous work was a triptych altar piece called *The Garden of Earthly Delights.* The right side of the triptych was a hellscape where mankind, having succumbed to temptation, reaped the rewards of eternal damnation. Near the middle of the painting, on the left side of the panel, a man lay facedown. A monster lashed him with its tongue, leaving a staff and a series of sixteen notes torn into the man's bare backside. The exact sequence of notes depicted in the painting was repeated three times in the first two pages of the composition.

After consulting some additional texts on another subject entirely, Harry put aside his reading and left, the cursed music and a single volume written in German tucked under his arm.

He had no proof. How could one prove the supernatural, after all? But somehow, Stearns had crafted a melody of shadows, designed to harm. Harry's course was set. When he reached the cottage, he would burn the pages.

His understanding of the universe was limited to three dimensions. Clearly, Mr. Newton's rules did not translate to other dimensions. Why would they? Planck's quantum theory postulated a completely different set of rules for the sub-atomic level. Harry whispered a line remembered from Shakespeare: "More things in heaven and earth, Horatio/than are dreamt of in your philosophy."

The road out of town offered precarious footing full of old snow and frozen ridges of mud. Trees cased in ice huddled against the wind. The dropping temperature chilled him, but the desolate winter vista worked its way into his mind as well as his bones.

He could not tie his strings of thought together. Elizabeth's heavenly piano interlude and the demonic sheet music of Alfred Stearns. Fourth dimensional representations of electromagnetic fields and the spiritual vortexes of mediums. Smiling neighbors clustered on Mrs. Hartley's lawn and the stern judgment of the Christmas Eve congregation. A cluster of Christmas roses and the shards of his best friend's skull buried in a trench wall. The blasted fields of France. The desolate road from New Concord. Above all else, the fear that his Elizabeth would be taken from him. *Everyone I've ever loved has died.*

Was there a variable to signify grace in the equation of his life? He began to shake.

The sound of tires crunching on snow alerted him to the automobile's approach. He stepped aside, but the car stopped alongside of him. "Professor? Mighty cold, eh? I saw you passing by. Can I drive you home?"

Harry nodded numbly. He climbed into the front seat. The man's full beard and smiling countenance was familiar. He'd been at the reception, but Harry didn't know his name. "Rich Miller," he said, offering a hand. "Fine of you to break up the winter with that wedding of yours." He put the auto in gear and pulled ahead. "The road's a mess. That's Ohio for you!" He glanced at Harry. "Like I said, I saw you passing the house and thought, that poor man needs a ride."

"Thank you," Harry said.

•　　•　　•　　•　　•

Mrs. Hartley agreed to stay through the night. Harry moved a chair and extra blankets into the bedroom. He left the door open and built up the fire, using the damned composition as kindling. He heated the meatloaf Mrs. Hartley had brought with her and served her a plate.

Elizabeth did not stir.

"I have to return to my workshop," Harry said. "I'm working on a cure."

A lie, but he had no intention of trying to explain himself. He put a hand to his wife's cheek. Her face was hot. Too hot.

Mrs. Hartley nestled into the chair as best she could. "I'll stay with her, Professor."

•　　•　　•　　•　　•

Elizabeth woke at daybreak. She tried to sit up but couldn't manage. Mrs. Hartley lay slumped in the chair, asleep. Elizabeth called out to Harry, but her voice was parchment. She had to go to the bathroom. She couldn't get up.

Harry came into the room, slow as a pallbearer. He leaned in to kiss her. She whispered her request, and he dipped his hands under her back, hoisting her into the air, dragging the blankets with him. He carried her as if she weighed nothing at all, and perhaps she didn't. She felt hollow inside. The fever hadn't broken.

After she'd made use of the bathroom, he carried her back to their bed. She lay her head against his shoulder, reveling in his warmth. "Stay and talk to me," she said.

"I must attend to poor Mrs. Hartley," he said. "But I'll spend the rest of the day here with you."

The carriage driver arrived shortly after. She heard Harry in the main room. "How is the new bed?" he asked.

"I slept soft and spoiled as a babe," the driver answered.

Mrs. Hartley, who'd awakened from her chair somewhat muddled, came to Elizabeth's bedside to say goodbye. When she was gone, Harry returned. He pulled the chair closer to Elizabeth's bed so that he could hear her.

"What happened to me?" she asked.

"I put you in danger," he said. "Do you remember looking at the sheet music?"

"I think so," she said.

"The music was dictated by a man using my machine. Because you can read music, you are able to imagine the notes. To hear them on the page. Stearns is—" Harry stopped, searching for the right word. "Stearns is mad. His song was an attack."

"Why?" Elizabeth asked.

"Perhaps he is like Iago from *Othello*. He hates for no reason, and so he attacks what is good and noble. Or perhaps he is pathologically envious. We are alive and he is dead. Either way, I was his dupe, and you were his victim." He rubbed his eyes. "I've burned the music."

"What have we done?" Her voice was very small. "Our device—"

"*My* device. You are not to blame."

"We both played a part," Elizabeth said. "Neither one of us would willingly serve evil." She paused, as if gathering strength for her next question. "Have we given voice to the damned, then? Are these the voices of demons?"

Harry shook his head. He seemed quite sure. "No."

"The thought occurred to you, though?"

"Yes."

Elizabeth tried to cough and couldn't.

Harry stood and left the room. He returned a moment later with a glass of water. She sipped it gratefully.

When she'd settled back on her pillows, he recounted what he'd discovered in the college library. "I am a scientist," he finished. "I do not believe in goblins. But I saw what the music did to you, and I discovered elements attributed to the supernatural in the composition. I must adjust my beliefs. The music was created to cause pain."

By now, the sun came through the window full strength. Her eyes hurt. Reminded of the bleeding, she turned away from him so he would not have to see her face.

"What's this?" he asked.

"I must be a horrible sight," she said, her voice trembling.

"Not possible," he said. "You could eat a full wheel of cheese and every loaf of bread at Albanesi's bakery. You could inflate like a balloon, and you would still be the most beautiful woman—"

"Stop, please."

He stopped.

They passed long minutes before she had control of her voice again. "You explained that you'd talked to four people. Who else?"

"Twelve, as of now," he said.

"When did you sleep last?"

He paused, and she wondered if he were considering a lie. But she would *know*. "The night before our wedding. No, the night before that."

"Oh, Harry! I can't see you clearly, but I can hear your voice. You have run yourself ragged."

He didn't answer.

"How were the others? Why didn't they warn you about this madman?"

No answer.

"You have a hypothesis. I know you do. Tell me what it is."

He cleared his throat. "During a particularly difficult birth, the baby—and certainly the mother—may suffer both physical and psychological trauma."

"Postpartum," she said. "I know of it. Midwives call it the *baby blues*."

Harry nodded absently. "For the child, leaving the close comfort of the womb for a wide world must be frightening." He scratched his unshaven chin. "I imagine that transitioning from a flesh-and-blood person to a spirit form would be much, much more horrifying. Disorienting. The five senses do not appear to operate as before."

"You seemed certain that you weren't speaking to . . . to damned souls."

"Quite certain," he said.

"How can you be so sure?" Despite her burning eyes and general weakness, fear was beginning to be eclipse these other discomforts. She licked her dry lips. "Harry?"

"I am certain because I spoke to our Mr. Brympton."

"Oh." Elizabeth sank back into her pillows.

"If any man was more deserving of paradise, I've not heard of him. He was the finest sort of person."

"How was Mr. Brympton? What did he tell you?"

Harry sighed. There was pain in the sound.

"What aren't you saying, Harry? You have a hypothesis," she repeated. "I'm your partner. You must tell me."

The cottage groaned. Snow on the roof, she guessed. She could hear her husband breathing unevenly.

"I wonder now if consciousness is an accident," he said at last. His voice was distant, as if he were talking to himself. "Five or six seconds that allows us self-knowledge. The soul might be comprised of particles that survive death, as Edison suspected."

"Life eternal?" Elizabeth encouraged.

"An accident."

"But what of God?"

"Perhaps God turned away for the blink of an eye and a millennium passed. Are we so flawed that he turned away, and left us to our own devices? I have no answers." He shrugged helplessly. "Years ago, the man who ran the U.S. Patent Office said that everything that could be invented had already been invented. Another bureaucrat, dreading paperwork, I suppose. But that is not how progress is made. Each scientific advance answers a question. But in the answering, two more questions arise." Harry leaned forward, his hands on the edge of the bed. "This machine answers one question and begs a *thousand* more."

"Tell me of poor Mr. Brympton."

When Harry spoke again, there were tears in his voice. "I believe that the transition from life to death affects people much the same as the war affected me." He paused. "Worse, I think. Like the worst cases. Catatonia. Dementia."

Elizabeth considered this. Shell shock. "Oh, no! What can be done?"

"You are aware of psychology, the study of behaviors. I obtained a copy of Wundt's *Beiträge zur Theorie der Sinneswahrnehmung*. He began his career in medicine, and he seems to take the science seriously, unlike some." He tried a small laugh and failed. "The book is in your library. I stole it from the college. I will return it, eventually." His voice trailed off.

"And the people you talked to on your device?"

"*Insanitatem*," he said.

Elizabeth began to weep. "How many of them, Harry?"

"I have only spoken to a dozen souls," Harry whispered. "I am not a doctor and I have no experience in the field of psychology."

"I know you, Harry Browning. I am asking questions that you've already asked yourself." She paused. Her throat was so dry! He seemed to know it and brought the glass of water to her lips again. When she could speak, she pressed him. "How did you proceed?"

She forced her eyes open. His shoulders were trembling. "I spoke to those I knew, believing that I could judge the person they were against their current state."

"And?"

"I could not speak to Drew. His soul may be trapped in France, in one of those bloody trenches."

"How many were insane, Harry? Tell me."

"Eight people is hardly a meaningful sample. And of those, I only knew my father and Mr. Brympton. Oh, and Mr. Hartley, the widow's husband—"

"How many went insane, Harry?" Her voice carried as much steel she could muster.

He sat back, his hands clasped in his lap. "All of them," he whispered.

"What?"

"All of them. Every last one."

•   •   •   •   •

Near dusk, Harry tried to feed some bone broth to Elizabeth, but she threw it up. He stripped the bed while she sat slumped in the chair. He covered her in fresh blankets before returning to the lab. "I'll be back soon," he promised.

She could feel herself slipping.

Something was eating her from the inside. She could lie to herself, but the truth was in her husband's tortured expression. Glistening eyes. Mouth struggling for a smile and collapsing in despair.

With the sun setting, her eyes ached less. She rocked her head back into the pillow and listened to Harry shout and curse through the closed door. At one point, she heard a crash and wondered if he'd taken a hammer to the machine.

•   •   •   •   •

When his outburst was over, he sat at the short bench on Elizabeth's chair, head in his hands. The Edison and Tesla machines lay in pieces on the floor. Harry hadn't broken his own device. He would not examine his reasons for sparing the machine.

Instead, he thought back to a conversation he'd had with Drew in the trenches, just before the shell landed. Harry remembered saying, "Death cannot be *solved*. Everyone dies."

"No," he said aloud. "*No!*" He surveyed the room. He'd been content here once, even happy for a short, glorious time. His machine. His workbench and tools. Four safe walls. Now, everything of substance had been revealed as an illusion. Mankind was caught in the current, a waterfall ahead. Death would be worse than the French hospital after the trenches. An eternity of worse. He'd not really allowed himself to consider the meaning of his own pronouncements. Now, the full horror struck him.

Elizabeth.

Harry returned to their bedroom, carrying a candle. The light made her turn away. Her breath came in shallow gasps. He said, "I am going to fetch the doctor."

"Should I take more medicine?"

Castor oil be damned, he thought. He would grab the doctor by the lapels and drag him back to the cottage if he had to. She would not leave him.

"Don't go, Harry." Her voice was paper thin. "If you leave, I don't know what will happen."

He set the candle on his bureau, far from the bed. "The doctor will be able—"

"The doctor will tell you there's nothing to be done. Stay, Love. I need you here with me."

"I've done this to you, Elizabeth," he said. "I must fix things."

"You can't," she said. "Please, Harry. Lie next to me. Hold me."

He rubbed his eyes with his palms. He felt as if his heart would burst.

"You know I'm right."

His shoulders shook. He could not speak.

"Please. Hold me." She lay shivering on her back, facing the ceiling.

He climbed onto the bed and wrapped an arm around her. Nestling close, he whispered, "Rest, then. I'll fetch the doctor in the morning when you're feeling better."

"Harry?"

"Yes, my Love?"

"I'm so frightened."

"I know," he whispered.

"I was never afraid of death before."

"Hush."

"Everything is different, now. I don't want to go insane. I don't want to lose myself." He could feel her body tighten under his arm. He started to answer, but cut himself off, burying his face in the crook of her shoulder.

The candle flickered on top the bureau, sending shadows dancing against the far wall. Harry watched the ballet of light and dark, all the while listening to Elizabeth fight for air.

Then, she stopped breathing.

He propped himself up on an elbow. Her mouth formed a perfect "o," cheeks pulling as if to draw in air. Her eyes, black in the gloom, grew wide with shock and then horror as if, having pitched face-first into a mine shaft, she saw the bottom rushing up to swallow her.

He watched in disbelief. Her body went still.

His Elizabeth was gone.

AFTER

The Man with the Prosthetic Jaw/
A New Endeavor

Berlin, 1922

The famous neurologist sits alone as the thin man stands wavering at the entrance to the café, a satchel in his hand. The café is a popular spot near the railway station. Berlin thrives, despite the war. People rush past, busy, some smiling. The thin man does not smile.

The café tables are covered in white linens. Ragtime music is playing. The Germans are cosmopolitan. They like swing and they are discovering jazz. The walls are covered with photographs of politicians and starlets. Dark paneled walls and large, sun-filled windows do battle. The neurologist thinks of good and evil. Here, the sunshine and white linens have won.

The thin man walks to the table and stands before the empty chair. "Herr Freud?" he asks.

The neurologist nods and gestures at the empty chair with his cigar.

When the thin man is seated, he launches into an introduction. "*Ich bin Harry Browning. Sandor Ferenczi hat mich an Sie verwiesen.*"

"Your German is excellent," the neurologist says. "I wonder if you would mind conversing in English? I would appreciate the practice."

The thin man nods. "I'm told you speak in several languages."

"Seven."

The thin man tries to smile. His lips twist the wrong way.

A waiter approaches. The neurologist says, "I have already ordered. Alas, our time is short. I have other obligations. Will you dine?"

The thin man glances down at a menu laid out before him. He orders a Thuringian bratwurst and a beer. When the waiter leaves, he begins to speak. "I am grateful for whatever time you can give me. How was my German accent?"

"Very American," the neurologist says. He tries to smile at his own joke, but his face feels wrong. He is engaged in a war with cancer. The prosthetic jaw renders his smile alien and robs him of the authoritative precision of speech that has been his trademark.

The thin man says, "As our time is short, may I ask my questions?"

The cigar answers him—a dip and a wave. *Begin.*

"The first question involves vaccines."

"Artificial activation of the immune system."

"My question involves the psyche. I wonder if a shell shock victim might be inoculated against further trauma by virtue of the earlier exposure."

The neurologist puffs his cigar. The thin man has posed an apples-to-oysters question. Clearly, the American does not know as much about the workings of the mind as his colleague Sandor suspected. "Let me answer you this way. Shell shock can be differentiated by cause. Physical damage to the brain will not prevent further physical damage—"

"I'm speaking of psychological trauma," the thin man says.

The neurologist purses his wet lips. He keeps his mouth closed, except when speaking, because the prosthetic embarrasses him. More, it is a constant reminder of mortality. He readies his answer, mentally, and then talks, his cigar hand in front of his face as a buffer. "Melancholia is distinct from mourning, in that the mourner refuses to decathect—to disconnect—from the object of loss. Sometimes, this refusal is tied to prior ambivalent feelings for the—"

"Melancholia is quite different from shell shock."

The cigar shows the man's irritation with a circular wave. "It's difficult to make subtle distinctions when the subject itself is suffused with misdirection. Many, if not most, cases of shell shock involve cowardice masquerading as anguish." The neurologist pauses, suddenly aware of the other man's physical state. He is painfully thin. His face has the hollow look of someone struggling internally. His eyes are dark and flat. Had this man battled shell shock himself? If so, then a great insult has been delivered, and that was not his intent. "I say this only because there has been very little study done in that area. Is that an application of the psychological sciences that interests you? My colleague tells me you have a remarkable mind."

The thin man glances away before continuing. "I am most interested in the treatment of severe psychological trauma. Psychotherapy interests me, as the application I have in mind must not, by necessity, involve machinery of any kind."

"No shock therapies? Why is that?"

"It's torture."

"I would hardly consider the electric cure to be torture."

"I can assume, then, that you've never experienced the procedure?"

The words hang over the table like a pendulum. The waiter carrying their plates dispels some of the tension. The thin man gazes at his bratwurst, covered in an onion-thyme sauce and served with parsley potatoes. He takes a single bite of sausage, followed by a single bite of potato. For the remainder of the meal, he shifts his attention to the beer.

The neurologist has selected a slice of meatloaf, topped with a fried egg. The loaf is moist, and easily chewed. At length, he says, "I find myself wondering why machines are not to be part of the treatment plan?"

"I will be treating Luddites." The neurologist notes the thin man's expression, and decides that he's just told a lie.

"Interesting," Freud says. "Well, then. I understand why you asked to speak to me. What behaviors are you hoping to change?"

"Not behaviors," the thin man says. "I hope to alter thoughts and emotions. To reestablish relationships."

"What sort of trauma is involved?"

"Death," the thin man says. He sips his beer. When he sets his mug back on the table, a thin line of foam rides his lip.

"Well," Freud says, waving his cigar. "That's definitive, I suppose." He is being sarcastic because the thin man offers little in the way of details. After a few moments of silence, he continues. "Have you experience with hypnosis?"

The thin man shakes his head. "I must restrict my efforts to socially authorized methods. The Luddites are a closed community. I am focused on the establishment of conversation rituals that will offer comfort."

"How will you analyze these conversations?"

"Analysis is secondary," the thin man says. "I need to establish a social framework for mutual benefit."

"Your Luddites sound like an aberrant bunch."

The thin man does not answer. His dark hair has a shocking strand of gray hair that begins at the upper corner of his left temple. His gaze reminds the neurologist of a fish. He does not blink. Perhaps the war profoundly damaged him.

"The value of having patients talk about themselves lies in interpreting the clues they provide. I encourage the patient to speak of their dreams, their childhoods. Psychoanalysis must, by its nature, involve analysis."

"Psychotherapy," the thin man says. His tone implies a correction. "I wish to establish a link between myself and the patient, to provide a framework for therapeutic inquiry."

"You seem to undervalue the role of the unconscious—"

"By focusing on the unconscious, you reduce the patient to a puzzle game."

The neurologist sits back, stunned by both the tone and substance of what has been said. He puffs on his cigar furiously. His meatloaf, suddenly unappealing, sits unattended. He is of half a mind to leave this American and his impertinent ideas to face the waiter's tab alone.

The thin man sways in his seat, as if he might pass out. He closes his eyes and rubs them with his thumb and index finger. After another sip of his beer, he mumbles, "I'm told we have a mutual admiration for the works of Shakespeare."

This sudden change in direction gives the neurologist pause. "Yes. When I was a younger man, I was interested in the works of Nietzsche and other philosophers. After my education in the field of neurology, I found more truth in the work of fictionalists."

The thin man nods with appreciation. "I concur. The Bard of Avon understood much about the mysteries of the human mind. You, sir, have done much to expand that understanding."

The neurologist recognizes two things. First, the substantive discussion is at an end. Second, the man in front of him wishes to part company as friends. This is a relief. He finds much to admire in this thin fellow. "I wonder," he says, "You speak English and German. What other languages have you learned?"

"Latin, Greek, French, and Spanish," he says. "Six in all. One less than you, sir." His deferential expression is punctuated with a bow and a hand over his heart. The neurologist suspects the man is lying—that he knows two or three more languages. If so, it's a charming lie.

.　　.　　.　　.　　.

The trip to Europe, far from the machine and the souls that gathered at the cottage, had been an exhausting necessity. During his travels, he met with great thinkers, including Freud, Ferenczi, and most importantly, Alfred Adler, whose individualistic approach to analysis struck Harry as a more realistic course of action for the problem at hand.

The machine would remain unchanged, without improvements or enhancements. His investigations into the realm of the physical sciences had ended. No more inventions. Instead, he would devote himself to an increased understanding of the human mind, with therapy as his goal.

He would not publicize his psychological theories, though any breakthroughs would surely have applications in the physical world. Time and death were his enemies, and he would not dilute his efforts with written treatises, peer defenses, and conference presentations. Every waking moment would be applied diligently to the task at hand.

When the time was right, he would publish his findings.

But the machine would be destroyed. Each night, he dismantled it, lest he die in his sleep. He'd already burned the journal containing Elizabeth's drawings. Stearns had killed her from beyond the veil. That capability must not fall into the hands of someone who might turn Harry's machine into a weapon.

These changes in his life's path did not bother him. That he would never learn to play the piano was a sole regret. Shortly after his return from France, he donated the instrument to the college.

Mrs. Hartley had arranged another housekeeper. Wilma was an older woman, nearly forty, with a stern lower lip that promised no nonsense. She kept Harry fed as best she could, though he had no lingering interest in food. She kept the house clean, except for the workshop and the library, where she was forbidden. Her husband was a carpenter, working on a project nearby. Each afternoon, he came for her in his tiny car—a "Red Bug," manufactured by the Briggs Stratton Company. The funny little vehicle looked like a sled with two seats. Come winter, electric motor on the fifth wheel would have trouble moving the car through the snow, and Harry would have to find some way of getting Wilma home. He supposed he would arrange a carriage.

Mrs. Hartley had contracted *Diabetes Mellitus*. Doctor Kemp, who had become interested in new treatments for disease, prescribed a fasting diet and exercise. The widow embraced the latter with enthusiasm, and the former with great reluctance.

Elizabeth had been buried alongside Harry's father—not in New Concord. The townspeople were surprised, and Harry's apparent disinterest in visiting the grave became a brief topic of gossip until his loss of weight, inability to smile, and general air of melancholy proved a satisfactory demonstration of grief.

For Harry, the grave meant nothing. His wife was elsewhere.

Though Harry's generosity to the collection plate made his presence a blessing for Pastor Frederick, Harry attended services irregularly. The building recalled his wedding, and every happy memory of Elizabeth had been colored like a daguerreotype—not in sepia, but in crimson.

Gradually, expectations for Harry's greatness and eventual fame dissipated, replaced by an understanding of his twin sorrows—war trauma and personal loss. Because he was viewed as a kind man, his flaws were ignored. The town held him in quiet regard. Shopkeepers tried to give him their wares, and men stopped to shake his hand. Wives whispered after him, wondering if their husbands would grieve so at their own passing.

·   ·   ·   ·   ·

At precisely five o'clock, Harry turns on the machine. Routine is an important part of the therapy he hopes to provide. He's spread out another sheet of butcher paper, ready for his notes. He has been dreading this moment, because talking to her gives birth to the worst sort of helplessness—a despair so profound that continuing day-to-day living seems impossible.

He does not have to call for her.

Harry:"Are you there?"

Elizabeth:"Yes. Yes, I'm here. I was so afraid you wouldn't come."

Harry:"I'm staying in New Concord from now on, I promise. The remainder of what I need to accomplish can be done by mail."

Elizabeth:"Will they write to you? The doctors? Can they help us?"

Harry:"I've established contacts, much as I did with the physical scientists. I will be kept abreast of any important studies."

Elizabeth:"I'm afraid. I'm so afraid."

Harry:"I'm here now."

Elizabeth:"But you will go away—"

Harry:"Not for hours. I am here with you now. And the others?"

Elizabeth:"You are surrounded by lost souls. And I am one of them."

Harry:"As long as we two can speak, you are not lost."

Elizabeth: [Voice breaking] "I can't bear this."

Harry:"You can. We will bear it together."

Elizabeth:"I can feel myself breaking apart."

Harry:"Talk to me, Elizabeth. Speak for yourself and for the people who can't speak."

Elizabeth:"They are dispersing. They are losing themselves. Only a few will talk to me."

Harry:"We will give them something to hold onto."

Elizabeth:"How can I give them anything? I have nothing left of myself."

Harry:"You were the first person to know, truly know, what was coming. You are still *you*."

Elizabeth:"I am all fear and static."

Harry:"When we talk, the fear recedes. You have said so."

Elizabeth:"But it returns!"

Harry:"Yes. It returns. But we will name the thing and make it smaller. We will find ways of mitigating the fear."

Elizabeth:"I miss you, Harry. I miss you so much."

Harry steps back for a moment, wiping away his tears. Each evening, he talks to her until physical and mental exhaustion leaves him drained. When he sleeps, he does not dream. He spends most of his time in bed staring at the ceiling. He knows every crack in the plaster by heart.

He takes a deep breath and returns to the task at hand.

Harry:"Words are our world now, so I will tell you how much I miss you. You will know that you are loved. I think of you in every quiet moment. I hear your echo in the rain, smell your skin where the dew rests."

Elizabeth:"You are speaking in poetics."

Harry:"Yes."

Elizabeth: "Don't stop. Your words are my anchor."

Harry:"When I lose patience, I think of you winding copper, and I can focus again. When I am too serious, I remember what you said about poor Mr. Edison's machine, and I smile."

Elizabeth:"You are lying. [Pause] You no longer smile."

Harry:"Do you see, Elizabeth? You *know* me. And I know you."

Elizabeth:"Yes."

Harry:"We will not lose that. Your mind, your soul, is still intact. And the things you've told me about the void have been helpful."

Elizabeth:"Yes. The void. [Static] trapped in amber and shadows. We are all afraid. It does no good to be afraid of the void, so we are afraid of each other instead."

Harry:"We will change that."

Elizabeth:"What if we fail? What if we are forever alone?"

Harry:"You said *we*. We can't be alone if we're together."

Elizabeth:"Can we really do this? Can this be done?"

Harry:"Yes. But first, we have work to do. I need you to be centered when I transition. I will *need* your help. You will keep me tethered to this new reality."

Elizabeth"How?"

Harry:"We will invent structure for the void."

Elizabeth:[Static] can communicate, but we're blind. No smell, no touch."

Harry: "I have other structures in mind. I've been thinking of bees. The honeycomb—the hexagon—is one of nature's perfect forms. The key to the afterworld is the establishment of community. I envision groups of six, supporting each other through communication rituals. Each group will be surrounded by six other groups, and so on." [Pause] "Of course, I wish I could be certain that what works for bees will work for souls."

Elizabeth:[Silence]

Harry:"Elizabeth?"

Elizabeth:"To bee or not to bee?"

The sudden laugh torn from Harry's throat is raw, and because it's coupled with tears, several moments pass before Harry can speak again. When he regains his voice, he says, "We will solve this problem. We will change the universe. We will be *together*, Elizabeth. Not soon enough—"

"—but forever?" Elizabeth asks.

The hint of hope in her voice, coupled with her small joke, is what he needs to continue. He dabs at his cheeks with his fingertips and thinks that she has flipped a switch inside him, completing a circuit, and though he is damaged, he is himself again. For the first time in months, he feels something like energy in his veins. "Yes. Forever."

"Let's begin, then."

With that, Harry Browning goes back to work.

ACKOWLEDGEMENTS

I want to take a moment to thank some people. I am in two critique groups (the Penpointers and the Raintree Writer), and the members gave me great feedback. Special thanks to cherished beta readers Ken Harmon and Pat Stoltey, and the best editor on the planet, Laura Mahal.

Additional thanks to Reagan Rothe, owner and creator of Black Rose Writing. The man is fearless.

Thanks to my very supportive wife Judith, who sat through about 700 rants and discussions on the way to boiling down the theme of my book to one brief sentence: "Love conquers almost all."

Finally, thanks to those who read my stories. This one was an odd combination of history, romance, horror and steampunk. I hope you enjoyed it.

Brian Kaufman

June 2022

About The Author

Brian Kaufman is a curriculum editor for an online junior college. By day, he writes textbooks on a number of topics, from business management and finance to HVAC repair. By night, he writes fiction, including eight published novels and a collection of novellas. Kaufman lives with his wife and dog in the Northern Colorado mountains, dividing his time between various passions, including writing, blues guitar, hiking, and book-hoarding.

Note From The Author

Word-of-mouth is crucial for any author to succeed. If you enjoyed *A Shadow Melody*, please leave a review online—anywhere you are able. Even if it's just a sentence or two. It would make all the difference and would be very much appreciated.

Thanks!
Brian Kaufman

We hope you enjoyed reading this title from:

BLACK ROSE
writing™

www.blackrosewriting.com

Subscribe to our mailing list – *The Rosevine* – and receive **FREE** books, daily deals, and stay current with news about upcoming releases and our hottest authors.
Scan the QR code below to sign up.

Already a subscriber? Please accept a sincere thank you for being a fan of Black Rose Writing authors.

View other Black Rose Writing titles at
www.blackrosewriting.com/books and use promo code **PRINT** to receive a **20% discount** when purchasing.